And Of Them Are True

Pam Barnard

k FOX

First published by Shakspeare Editorial, December 2020

ISBNs   hbk 978-1-8383041-2-6
            pbk 978-1-8383041-0-2
            ebk 978-1-8383041-1-9

Copyright © 2020 Pam Barnard

No part of this publication may be reproduced, stored in a retrieval system, or transmitted, in any form or by any means mechanical, electronic, photocopying, recording or otherwise without the prior written consent of the publisher; nor be otherwise circulated in any form of binding or cover other than that in which it is published and without a similar condition being imposed on the subsequent purchaser.

The right of Pam Barnard to be identified as the author of the work has been asserted by her in accordance with the Copyright, Designs and Patents Act 1988.

Design and typesetting www.ShakspeareEditorial.org

Author photo: Mike Brett
Cover photo: Kyo Azuma, unsplash.com

Contents

1. Introducing Joanne 1
2. A Pair of Marked Hands 3
   Snapshot 1 ✽ 21 10
3. Crossing the Channel 11
4. Berlin Corridors 20
5. College Corridors 30
6. School Corridors 35
   Snapshot 2 ✽ Measuring 41
7. Beside the Seaside 42
8. Fig Rolls 52
   Snapshot 3 ✽ Voyages to Camelot 59
9. Tasting Figs 60
10. Platform 1 67
11. Platform 2 73
12. Platform 3 80
13. Tugged and Splintered 89
14. Several Cycles 98
    Snapshot 4 ✽ Sunday School 106
15. Give Me a Mask 107
16. Writing Lessons 114
    Snapshot 5 ✽ Family Words 124
17. Meeting Three Poems 125
18. First Infant 137
19. Second Infant 142
20. Finding Elisabeth Ann 147
21. Making Homes 157
22. Playing Tennis 163
23. Endnotes 169

Introducing Joanne

I tell these stories through the character of Joanne. She is not me, yet some of her perceptions are like mine, but not all. Her personality from pre-school to old age follows my journey, but selectively.

I can only write about what I know, so some parts of my stories are true in the sense that they happened. I wonder if my readers can guess which episodes they are?

***

I am grateful to my gentle editor, Geoff, and my valued writing partner, Anne. You both encouraged and helped me to move from scrappy anecdotes and sketchy observations to stories with some shape and voice.

Thank you both.

A Pair of Marked Hands

'He'll be scarred for life,' said Mother, who'd just taken her three-year-old son to Sick Quarters.

'I don't care,' thought Joanne, as she carefully licked the chocolate off a Mars bar to postpone the fudgy delight underneath.

Her brother was blond, blue-eyed and allergic to everything except Weetabix and custard. His soft pale skin would 'erupt', that was Mother's word, into batches of spots if he ate porridge, tomatoes, beef stew, rice pudding; anything, in fact, that Joanne liked. He was so annoying to his sister, and so demanding of his mother who celebrated his irritating ways, such as trailing lengths of her old silk nightdresses up to bed to soothe him to sleep. He didn't have to contend with malevolent spiders in the corner of a bedroom, intent upon crawling over a sleeping face when the light was out. He was looked after.

The day had begun with the breakfast fight. Mother had poured the top-of-the-milk over Joanne's cereal.

'I wanted that on my Weetabix,' complained Paul.

Joanne scraped a creamy teaspoonful of hers and put it on Paul's.

'Ugh, ... sicky,' his face screwed up.

'Look, I gave you the best bit. The cream.'

'Sicky, ugh ... Muuum.'

Paul's cry expressed the leg-pinch she'd given him.

Later, in the park, Joanne commandeered the swing with its wooden seat (much hacked by penknives) and its rough hairy ropes. Working her legs, she was swinging higher and higher, her Mother and Paul wandering away under the trees. She closed her eyes and dreamed her favourite dream: being a princess who wore long dresses and high heeled sling-back shoes.

The swing was subsiding, so Joanne leaned backwards with her eyes closed and feet straight out. At the peak of the swing, she curled her legs in and leaned forwards. Down she swung and prepared for the next impetus. Legs stretched out, she caught sight of her brother stomping across the grass worn down by other swingers. She didn't retract her legs. Her sandals caught her brother's back. Down he went and the screaming started.

'What did you do that for?' she was asked after the screams had reduced. 'And look, he's cut his hand.'

True enough, there was a long deep gash across his palm and it was bleeding quite a lot. Mother's handkerchief was bound around it and Paul was told to keep his hand touching his shoulder.

'What a fuss,' thought Joanne.

They got into the blue and grey Riley. Him sitting in the front, of course. The cracked leather seats itched her legs, but worst of all was the smell of the car itself, metallic and sickly. It always made her feel woozy. The distinctive engine note whined up and up as Mother changed gears with a lever near the steering wheel.

Paul was consoling himself in the front seat by rubbing a scrap of his mother's old nightdress in his shorts' pocket: 'Silking,' the family called it. That was allowed, but Joanne was not permitted to bite her nails, even though she'd given up sucking her thumb.

Back home, Joanne was left in the care of the National Service batman, who was using the bumper to polish the brown lino floor of the kitchen, swinging the heavy felted head hinged to its handle backwards and forwards.

'I'll polish the buttons on the Squadron Leader's uniform before I go. You'll be back by then with the wee chap,' the Scottish voice said.

'Of course. I'll ask if the medic will see him straightaway. Don't be a nuisance, Joanne, and don't ask Jock your everlasting questions.'

Joanne heard the Riley pull away from the Married Quarters as she went to raid the sultana jar in the pantry. Time to read *The Magic Faraway Tree* and think of where she'd like to be: far away from her pesky brother.

He came back, of course, with a huge white bandage round his bad hand and a new Dinky car in the other.

'Typical,' thought Joanne. She wouldn't have minded being 'scarred for life' for, say, a doll's tea set or, better still, a junior tennis racquet.

***

Hundon School was an all-age village school, late-Victorian in style, unadapted to the 1950s and located in rural Suffolk. Joanne's father had been posted to a nearby RAF station, where he was in charge of the control tower and the station's fire-service. Unlike most officers' children, Joanne went to this local all-age school.

It was awful in her view. The building had large classrooms, big enough for fifty children, pitted asphalt playgrounds, and outside hole-in-wooden-seat-with-bucket lavatories that smelled foul. Joanne quickly learnt to hold herself in all day and to run home from the camp bus.

Changing schools was something she'd done many times, learning to be friendly, but not too visible. The 'big girls' in the school came from the village and wore headscarves in the playground, where they gossiped and nodded like grown-ups.

One day, lining up for school dinners, Joanne found herself next to three of the big girls.

'Have you washed your hands?' the fair-haired one demanded.

'Yes,' said Joanne, affronted. 'Have you?'

'Of course,' said Blondie, giving a grown-up sniff.

'Well, what's that on your hands, then?'

'What do you mean? My hands are perfectly clean.'

Joanne could see that was not strictly true and, being a literalist, said, 'Look, they've got brown marks all over them.'

'That's walnut stains from our tree.'

'Yes, but,' the literalist persisted, 'that's still dirt marks.'

The three big girls moved closer. One tightened her headscarf and another sniffed loudly.

The third said, 'Who d'you think you're talking to, squirt? Are you saying my cousin's dirty, eh?'

'No, but stained hands are actually dirty hands, aren't they?'

Joanne's logic was lost on the village girls.

'Just you wait 'til tomorrow and you'll see who'll be dirty all over ... in the school lavatories. The teachers can't see us there.'

Joanne realised she had gone too far.

As soon as she got home – after peeing for England – Joanne asked her mother if she could have two weeks' pocket money before Saturday because she needed to get some school stuff from the NAAFI. She bought a pencil sharpener of the metal kind that everyone wanted, an ink eraser and a big KitKat bar.

The next day the camp bus parked outside the metal gates of the school. Joanne got out, unbuckling her satchel, and pulling out the brown-paper bag with its three treasures. The three big girls stood by the wall with their headscarves knotted under their chins. Their arms were folded.

'Well ... who's got a brown-paper bag in her dirty little hands?' demanded the fair-haired one.

'I thought you might like these,' said Joanne, proffering the bag. It was grabbed without a word.

'Aren't you going to say sorry, too?'

'I'm sorry. They were marks on your hands, not dirt.'

The three big girls sniffed in unison and stomped off to their class. Joanne, meanwhile, went through the middle door to Mr White's classroom, past his high desk with its row of worn tennis balls to be thrown unerringly at anyone whose head was turned away to talk to a neighbour.

At 12:30 there were school dinners. Joanne hated them. They tasted odd and the all-too-frequent stew had strange ingredients. Joanne had already told her doubting mother about the thin strands of grass she saw in the thick brown gravy. The tables had to have five girls and five boys. Two older girls served everyone and woe betide anyone who said they didn't want cabbage or the oddly flavoured mashed potato. They gave you double. Boiled potatoes often flaked onto the wooden tables and eagle-eyed boys would quickly flick the lumps onto the jumper of the girl opposite.

The only good things about the dinner hour were the stories her friend, Jane, daughter of a warrant officer, told her about her life. Jane told Joanne her biggest secret one day: she was really a Russian princess. Joanne asked her how she knew. Jane said she had a precious locket that had photographs of her real father and real mother. He had a black beard and she wore a diamond tiara in her dark plaited hair. They were, Jane said, true Russian nobility and she was, too, and her secret name was Anastasia. Another sign of royalty, Joanne was told, were delicate white hands and blue veins on the inner wrist.

'See,' said Jane, taking off her mittens and turning her clean pale hands over. True, she did have blue veins. In the bath later that night Joanne looked at her own wrists with great care ... she, too, had noble blood.

All too soon the oldest boy would walk round the playground ringing the large handbell for everyone to line up for the classrooms. The long afternoon lay ahead. No stories in Mr White's class, just sums, reading aloud round the class, and handwriting practice with dip-pens whose nibs crossed easily and splattered ink across the page, and no talking.

Another two hours before the relief of home.

Snapshot 1
21

The Old Mill Hotel on the River Stour was the venue for Joanne's twenty-first.

They thought that was the only dangerous part of the slow-flowing river.

When they were children, they'd paddled away from its deeps, summer dresses tucked into knickers, Clarks' sandals abandoned on the bank with white socks, printed with yellow patterns from buttercup pollen.

The children splashed and shouted. The bridge echoed their sounds and fork-tailed birds skimmed the water.

'Hey! You children. Come out of there. Now.' A grown-up was silhouetted against the sun.

'Why? It's fun!'

'Spoilsport!' they shouted, safe in the water up to their knees.

'Don't you know? Haven't you heard? Didn't your parents tell you?'

'What?'

'What?'

'Donald's in hospital, poliomyelitis. He paddled in the river just last week.'

Donald never reached 21.

Crossing the Channel

The two children held on tight to their mother's gloved hands. She had told them that this was going to be a big adventure.

'Just like the one Rupert Bear and Tiger Lily had?' Joanne had asked.

'Well, not quite,' Mother said, handing their passports to the uniformed man who'd been drumming his fingers on the barrier.

'But they did go on a big boat to escape the wizard,' Joanne insisted.

Mother sighed; Joanne's recall of storylines suffered from much blending and an overemphasis on wolves.

Daddy had been posted to Berlin in 1948 – 'Control Tower duties,' he'd said – and they were to join him: Harwich to Hook of Holland; train to Hanover; overnight in a services' rest centre; and on by train through the Russian-occupied zone to Berlin.

'There are lots of wolves in Russia,' Joanne had told little brother, Paul. Even that news didn't make him remove his thumb from his mouth as they walked up the gangplank.

The ship was large, grey and staffed by servicemen with lists and stubby pencils.

'Yes, Mrs Ebrington, you and the children will be in bunks in 49B, second deck. You have got your overnight case, haven't you?'

The ship smelled cabbagy, or something worse. 49B proved to be a large cabin with triple-tiered bunks and one porthole.

When they found the cabin, one of the bottom bunks had already been commandeered by a large lady with bright red hair and, to Joanne's ear, a funny way of talking. Mother said, 'Sssh, she's Irish.'

'Oh, isn't he a pet?' The lady patted Paul on the head. He blinked his long-lashed blue eyes and Joanne smiled at the lady. He, of course, would have the bunk above Mother and Joanne would have to climb the ladder to the top bunk.

'Is your husband an officer too? Mine's a warrant officer and he's been in the Gatow camp three months in charge of the aircraft engineers.'

Joanne could hear Mummy's 'posh voice' as she replied, 'Well, my husband is a squadron leader. He's based in the city.'

'My husband says only the Yanks fly in and out of the city and that special transport planes bring their families fresh milk every day.'

'Oh, does he? Joanne, stop teasing Paul and get undressed while I take him to the bathroom.'

'My, your mother's a quiet one, isn't she?' A question of the kind that grown-ups asked that Joanne didn't know how to answer but, anxious to defend her mother, she said, 'Mummy hates boats.'

'Goodness me. Why's that, I wonder?'

Joanne had nearly trapped herself into revealing her mother's non-swimmer fears. 'I don't know. I think their smell might make her feel sick.' Joanne's car-travel experiences saved her mother's secret.

'I pee'd in a funny potty full of sand,' Paul announced as he opened the cabin door.

'The bathroom was busy, so we used a fire-bucket,' Mother explained to the Irish lady and Joanne giggled.

'Now into bed both of you. And try to go to sleep.'

And then the ship's engines started. They juddered mightily and the tall bunks shook.

'I guess we're leaving harbour,' the Irish lady said, 'Time for a snifter, as my husband would say. I'm sure he won't mind us trying a little of his very favourite port.'

Joanne didn't know what a snifter was but from her mother's expression it wasn't something nice.

From out of a small brown case, the Irish lady pulled a pink silky-looking nightdress, a pair of high-heeled fluffy slippers, a large bottle of browny-red liquid and a collapsible green plastic cup just like the one Joanne's Grandma had bought from The Ideal Home Exhibition.

'Do you drink port at all Mrs … ?'

'Not really, and my surname is Ebrington.'

The Irish lady sat on her bunk and from her handbag produced an impressive Swiss Army knife. Joanne watched as she selected the corkscrew, levered the cork, which popped out quietly, and filled her plastic cup.

'Cheers and bottoms up!' she said.

Mother left the cabin saying, 'I'm just going to the bathroom, children.'

Joanne could smell the fruity drink. It made her think of last Christmas when Daddy was home on leave, 'I'll see you soon, Droopy Drawers,' he'd said when he left the next day, giving her a tickly kiss with his moustache. She hated him calling her Droopy Drawers. It was rude.

Mother returned. The Irish lady was pouring herself some more browny-red drink.

'Are you sure you won't have some, Mrs Ebrington? It's very good for the seasickness, I believe.'

'No thank you, Mrs …?'

'Call me Colleen. Most people do.'

Mother set about preparing herself for bed while the Irish lady renewed her drink several times.

'Would you ever believe my husband and me have only spent a fortnight together since we were married in the spring?'

'Oh, really. But that's service life for you.'

'He says you don't need to go into Berlin at all since there's a good NAAFI on the camp at Gatow.'

'I dare say there is. Well, good night, Mrs … '

'Colleen. Please call me Colleen. They say Berlin is bombed out; a dreadful place, what with the Russians all around.'

Mother put out their bunk lights and Joanne could see the Irish lady drinking and hear her humming a sad-sounding tune. Then the cabin began to move up and down and sideways all at once. Mother took some tablets and got into her bunk. Joanne peeped through her lashes.

The Irish lady started moaning and hiccupping, then saying something that made no sense to Joanne about mothers and cods. Joanne closed her eyes and hoped she wouldn't dream about wolves.

***

The tannoy bell woke them all up with, 'Good morning everyone. We disembark in half an hour. Please make your way to the lower deck in good time.'

'Joanne, get up and use the bathroom while I get Paul ready, will you?'

There was no light through the porthole and Mother was looking rather strange.

'Where's the Irish lady?' Joanne asked, seeing the brown suitcase open on the opposite bunk as the boat lurched and an empty bottle rolled out from underneath the bunk.

'Goodness knows. Now get yourself going, please, Joanne.'

'She took her Swiss Army knife with her wherever she is. I'd like one of those for Christmas. Can I add it to my list?' said Joanne, opening her new leather shoulder bag.

'Not now, Joanne. Just go and clean your teeth.'

'Can I use Paul's Punch and Judy toothpaste, please?'

'Very well. Now get a move on for goodness sake.'

Once they'd got organised, they climbed the steep narrow stairs following a long line of grown-ups and a few children. Each person, grown-up or child, was asked their name, and the lists were checked again. Joanne wondered why, because no one could get on or off a boat as it crossed the Channel so the lists must still be right.

They stood about while the boat steered nearer and nearer to the dark dockside. With a gentle bump, it stopped.

'We're here at last, children,' said Mother, 'The Hook of Holland. We'll soon be on the train, I hope.'

'Calling Mrs Colleen Hillscombe. Mrs Hillscombe, please report to the checking desk on the upper deck.'

'Mummy, is that the Irish lady from our cabin? She said her name was Colleen.'

'It could be. I'm sure I don't know.'

'Only, when she stopped singing last night, she said something about feeling a bit sick. That's when she went.'

Mother just sighed and stroked Paul's hair. The ship still smelled of cabbage, and one of the grown-ups said, 'You'd think they'd give us some breakfast, wouldn't you?'

Just then the tannoy announced, 'Due to a delay in disembarkation, tea and toast are available downstairs in the buffet area, ladies and gentlemen. Please make your way there in an orderly fashion.'

Mother took the children's hands. As they duly made their way, a uniformed man with three silver stripes on his sleeve, called out, 'Mrs Ebrington? Mrs Ebrington, can you identify yourself and come to the upper deck?'

'Oh, bother,' said Mother. 'Just when I thought I'd at least get a cup of tea. Excuse me ... sorry ... excuse me, please.'

They climbed up the narrow stairs when everyone else was going down.

'Ah, you must be Mrs Ebrington and you must be Joanne and Paul. That's right, isn't it?'

'Yes,' said Joanne, 'We are.'

'Sshh, Joanne, let Mummy speak.'

Joanne could see that Mother still looked strange and a little wobbly, as Grandma would have said.

'Ah, Mrs Ebrington. You shared a cabin last night with Colleen Hillscombe.'

'Yes, we did.'

'Well, she has just been found asleep behind a lifeboat in the stern. The family officer has talked to her and he says that she is very apprehensive about the journey to Berlin through the Occupied Sector ... she's also a bit the worse for wear, if you know what I mean.'

'Yes, I do.'

'But I don't. Mummy, what is wrong with Mrs Colleen?'

'Shush Joanne, and let me talk to the officer ... Is that it, can we go now?' as Mother pulled Paul away from the rails and picked up the overnight bag.

'Just a minute, please, Mrs Ebrington. The family officer has asked whether you, as the wife of a senior officer, would mind taking Mrs Hillscombe under your wing, as it were? She said she'd be much comforted if she could travel in your carriage and share sleeping accommodation in Hanover until you reach Berlin.'

'Oh, I see.' Mummy sighed.

'That'll be lovely, Mummy, won't it? She might show me all the things her Swiss Army knife can do and she has a very pretty nightdress and lovely fluffy slippers.'

The officer coughed and shook Mother's hand, 'Mrs Hillscombe is waiting on the main deck with the family officer. Thank you for your understanding, Mrs Ebrington, and bon voyage, as our French friends say.'

The children took Mother's hands and the three carefully climbed down the stairs to the main deck. They checked into the crowded train carriage.

''Tis lovely to see you, Mrs Ebrington, and you too, pet. I thought a bottle of port would be good on the journey, see. It's not my husband's favourite port but getting any from that miserable bar steward was a near miracle.'

'Mmm,' said Mother.

The train whistled and exhaled its steam. At last it felt as though they were on their way to Berlin.

Berlin Corridors

1948

The blinds were down as the three sat in a sleeping compartment of the train to Berlin. Uniformed men patrolled the corridors to ensure no one could see out and no one could see in. Documents were checked and, from the children's perspective, everyone had been shushed. But why?

No explanation was given, so Joanne, the eldest, whispered to her brother, 'I bet it's the Russians!'

Paul, at three, was oblivious to the international situation and Joanne, aware of something dangerous in Europe, had an image of bearded giants in high snowy boots accompanied by wolves, another of her persistent fears.

The train moved on and at long, long last reached a big station in Berlin where Daddy, in uniform, was waiting with his driver.

'We've got a third-floor flat ... quite big ... a garden for the children. We'll get a proper house when the CCG can find it,' he told Mummy.

The magic of initials intrigued Joanne; somehow they suggested secrecy, strength and grown-up business. She began to mutter 'CCG, CCG' before she went to sleep that night as a warning to the wolves that stalked through her dreams.

In the morning, Inge had arrived and she gave the children breakfast.

'She's our maid,' said Mummy.

Paul ate his Weetabix slowly.

'Milk, uurhg!' he spluttered.

'Well, you'll have to get used to it. It's the only kind we've got.'

Joanne understood that some things were going to be very different: a maid, tinned milk and a new school. The school bus collected her from the end of the road. Of course, she knew no one and, she quickly learnt, she was the only 'services kid' in that school as the RAF station was on the edge of the city at Gatow and had its own school.

A long drive led to the large building, which looked to her a bit like Buckingham Palace. That was her school. It had a big hallway with a wide, curved staircase and a huge globe that could be turned faster and faster if no teachers were around. There was a large gymnasium with wall bars to hang upside down from, a wooden balance bar to teeter across, and ropes that she could never scale. The playground was grass that sloped towards the River Spree; in summer to roll down, in winter to sledge down.

Morning milk was made bearable by a stir of cocoa if you said, 'heist, bitte'.

The corridors were confusing. Finding the right classroom was a challenge for the first week. But even longer corridors baffled her at Brownies. The British Berlin Pack met at the Olympic Stadium. She was a 'fairy', the badge sewn on to her brown uniform with its yellow tie. Brownies was like school, only worse, with lots of lining up, teams, instructions and hundreds of badges to be won, involving hours of tasks to be done at home. The only good bit was when they all escaped down the long marble corridor populated by statues of naked sportsmen. Some of the Brownies would stop every week to study the discus thrower.

'Look, he's got a bare willie. It's rude, isn't it?' said Rosemary.

'My brother's got a waggler,' boasted Joanne. 'I see it in the bath.'

But no one was interested.

At school the next day, talk was about The Russians.

'They've got tanks and they do exercises in the streets. They can come down any road. No one can stop them,' one of the boys stated.

Joanne hoped they would move soon from their flat in its wide street to a road so narrow that a tank would get stuck at the end. Soon after, they did move to a smaller street, to a house that was square, with lots of windows, a basement with a drive-in garage, an attic with a playroom each for Paul and herself, and, strangest of all, what Mummy called 'a zinc-lined fur cupboard' that the children weren't to play in. Joanne explored it; it was cold and dark and totally empty. For some reason, it made her shiver.

All around the house were bombed buildings. Their house stood handsome but alone.

'Bombed buildings are dangerous,' said Mummy, 'So don't play near them.'

Instead, play involved fighting with Paul, going with Mummy to swim at the Blue-White Club, or spending time with the American boy who lived at the end of the street. He had a collection of 'dangerous comics', as Joanne thought of them. She read them avidly, drawn by frightening images of monsters, volcanoes, dark, dark dungeons with implements of torture and, worst of all, Russians hunting with wolves.

One night she woke screaming from being chased by those wolves and Russians. Daddy listened to her account of the 'wolf noise', a relentless beating in her ears, and her worries about the Russians, their tanks and boots.

'Look, Joanne, down the corridor at the Air Safety Centre is the Russian Officer I work with to keep the air corridors safe. Would you like to meet him?'

'No, thank you, Daddy.'

'All right but when you're ready ... just say. He's a nice chap, really.'

Playing in the garden one day, making moss-nests for fairies to sleep in, Joanne heard, 'Pssst, English

Girl!' The words were repeated louder and came from the fence at the bottom of the garden.

Cautiously, she walked past the cabbages, grown by Hans, the boilerman and gardener. She saw three children, a tall boy, a girl the same size as her, and a little girl, holding their hands.

'Hello, English Girl,' the boy said.

'Ich canisch sprenke sei deutch,' Joanne replied.

'Your name?'

'Joanne. What's yours?'

'Gunter. Come. Play, if you please.'

She climbed over the fence and followed them through the rough remains of a neighbouring garden. Near a broken brick wall, the children had made a den, with planks on bricks for seats and a table. There were dock-leaf plates with grass seeds for food. The children sat down and pretended to feast, laughing like grown-ups and playing at drinking heavy mugs of beer.

'Berliner Kindle,' they said. 'Ein, Swei, Zuffer!'

Joanne enjoyed their jolly game and the lack of questions. She'd had plenty of those at school.

'What does your father do?' ... 'Why are you not at the school in Gatow with the other services' children?'

'Joanne, supper-time!' She heard Inge's voice call.

'Auf wiedersehn,' she said to the friendly children and sped off. 'Coming, Inge,' she shouted as she scrambled over the fence.

Each week on a Saturday Joanne met Gunter and his sisters on the other side of the fence. They played games of cowboys and indians, and, more frighteningly, 'The Russians are coming'. That game required hiding while one of them, usually Gunter, strode about shouting, 'Wo sind sie?' and 'where are you?' And, 'I will shoot you when I see you and feed you to my wolves.'

Finding new places to hide got more difficult for the girls. They were getting nearer and nearer to the forbidden bombed-out house in the middle of the wrecked garden. On the fourth Saturday of the game, Joanne wrenched open the door that was down an incline at the side of what she guessed was once a house like hers. She thought it would reveal a half-cellar like they had. There were concrete steps part-covered with rubble and they led downwards. That was OK; there would be narrow windows to let in light. Joanne pulled the door shut and the three girls stood there.

'We go down more,' said the older sister, Gertrude. And they did.

The girls could hear Gunter shouting and scrabbling about on the rubble stacked at the side of the house against what remained of the side wall. Then there was a rumble and another rumble then a cry of 'Damnation!' from Gunter.

All went quiet.

'We go now?'

'Ja, I think so,' replied Joanne.

They made their way up the steps, stumbling and slipping. There were no half windows and the only light came from the jagged top of the closed cellar door.

'We give in, Gunter. You can shoot us dead,' conceded Joanne.

There was no reply. The girls shouted his name, still no reply, so they pushed on the door. 'We'll put our hands up. We give in,' but the door wouldn't move.

Little sister began to cry. Gertrude cuddled her. Joanne started to explore, feeling her way down the steps through the pitch dark. She got to a level surface and edged her wellingtons forward. Suddenly her foot hit something that slid forward with a scraping noise. Stretching out her arms she felt a horizontal handle supported by curved metal struts. She felt downwards to rubber-covered wheels and upwards to a shiny-textured box: a doll's pram. She'd asked St Nicholas for one of those in her letter before his visit on December Fifth but all she got was a bag of sweets 'for being a good girl'. She wondered if the lucky girl who'd had this pram had been extra-specially good but, maybe, she hadn't been that lucky. Her house had been bombed to smithereens, leaving only the cellar and piles of bricks.

'Where are you?' came the cry from Gertrude. 'My sister doesn't like this game,' and the little sister whimpered loudly.

Joanne didn't like this game either. Where was Gunter? Was he too frightened to ask a grown-up to rescue them from where they shouldn't be? Time was moving on, according to her Timex illuminated-dial watch, and still no one came. Apart from little sister's whimpers, all she could hear was the sound of dripping water and Gertrude's gentle and perpetual coughs.

To cheer themselves up, Joanne started to sing 'Oh Tannenbaum', a Christmas song they had been taught at school for the parents' show. Gertrude joined in, then came the piping voice of little sister. They were on their third version when they heard the voices of men, calling 'Girls! Girls, where are you?'

'Down here! In the cellar! We're down here,' shouted Joanne.

They could hear the scraping of boots on bricks, grunts and mutters, and Gunter's voice saying, 'We play here ... together. It's good together, English girl and German children.'

Then there was a sound of the cellar door being wrenched and suddenly a shaft of light shone down at the girls, who stopped singing. They blinked and could see nothing but brightness. As their sight adjusted, Joanne could see three man-shapes and one boy-shape outlined against the sun. Gradually, she made out Daddy, Hans and Gunter, but who was the other grown-up in a dark uniform?

'I take sisters home,' announced Gunter.

'All right,' said Daddy. 'Just don't fall into any bomb craters! And thank you for fetching us.'

Walking up the tangly garden and onto the road, going the proper way back to their house, Joanne puzzled about the stranger. His uniform was different from Daddy's. He smiled at her but said nothing through his black moustache, much bigger than Daddy's.

Inge met them at the door and took their coats and outdoor shoes. Mummy rubbed Joanne's cold hands and, unusually, gave her a hug.

'Well,' said Daddy, 'Aren't you going to say thank you to the rescue team? The ones who prevented an international incident through close cooperation and mutual understanding.'

Joanne couldn't understand why Daddy was talking like this, sounding like the CCG news on the radio. She looked down at her feet and mumbled, 'Thank you for rescuing me,' to Hans, Daddy and the smiling stranger.

Then her hand was taken by the stranger and her chin was lifted up, 'I am not Ivan the Terrible. I am Ivan, your Daddy's corridor friend ... and I have no snowy boots on, no wolf to hunt with, and no tank to drive up your road.'

Joanne felt embarrassed that her secret fears were known by this officer-stranger. She mumbled thank yous again and looked upwards. He had put on his cap with its metal badge and his black gloves. He was even taller than Daddy and his eyes smiled at her.

'Now you can visit the Air Safety Centre to see your Daddy and me, and our friends Pierre and Hank at work, and not be frightened.'

'I shall,' said Joanne, suddenly feeling brave. 'And I shall see the air corridors for myself.'

'Oh, there's nothing to see really, Joanne,' said Daddy. 'Just some maps with lines and the radar blips of planes.'

'And empty coffee cups and biscuit crumbs,' added Ivan.

Joanne carefully hid her disappointment. She'd imagined air corridors as big tubes like huge long balloons, guarded by blimps, with Allied planes flying along them to safe landings at Templehof or Gatow.

Ivan's driver started the car. She waved to Ivan all the way down the street, then went to find Paul for another round of their sibling wars in the attic.

College Corridors

Joanne chose which college she would apply to in a fit of pique.

In the spring term of 1960 the grammar school sixth form sat in the library awaiting the arrival of the Headmaster for their weekly dose of 'breadth in the curriculum'. There were only thirty in the whole two-year cohort, more boys than girls. They were the remainder from each year's intake of sixty to make two forms: A and B. No B-group members ever stayed on after O-levels and only half of the A stream did, mostly those chosen to study Latin after the second year.

Joanne was deemed 'a good all-rounder': in sports teams, the upper A stream, and socially confident. The Head's enrichment lesson this day was on politics. He began by asking, 'Does anyone know what proportional representation means?'

Most of the Head's questions evoked silence, but Joanne put up her hand and gave an answer. Instead of the expected grave nod, the Head asked how she knew about such matters. Joanne said that some of her cousins were Methodists and Liberals who favoured PR.

'Mmmn, an odd explanation,' was his response.

A feeling of belittlement swept over her. A boy's voice muttered, 'Not so clever-clogs'. Angry, she stood up and walked out of the room just before she burst into tears.

An hour later, she was summoned to the Headmaster's study.

'Why did you walk out of my lesson, Joanne?'

The sun illuminated him in profile; long hooked nose and a bush of curly hair.

'I didn't want to cry in front of the others, sir.'

'So, you were upset about something?'

Joanne permitted herself a nod. There was a pause as the junior-boys' soccer team clattered past the window.

'I expect you're thinking about what you'd like to do next, when you leave, are you?'

Another nod.

'I understand you want to go to teacher training college.'

No nod.

'I think that's ideal for you ... a good all-rounder. And when you marry you can pick up teaching after children, and the holidays are good, too. A training college is ideal for you.'

No nod.

'You don't seem sure. You don't want to go to university, do you?'

Silence. Then an unwilling, 'No, sir, not really.'

'I tell you what, just to show you that you could have gone, had you chosen, I'll put you in for a County Major Award ... if you get the offer, you'll know you were, in fact, quite good enough to have gone to university.'

The black telephone rang, he answered and waved Joanne out of his study. And that was that.

A month later, Joanne was interviewed in London's County Hall for a place in an A-group mixed teacher training college in south London. She was accepted and duly, in late summer, the A-level results came. Her total marks met the requirement of a County Major for fees and grants at university. She had not, of course, made any applications for a place.

Preparations for college were simple. A second-hand trunk was bought to send on ahead and two suitcases were packed to carry up to Paddington, on the tube to Charing Cross, and then on a suburban line to south London. Finally, there was a short taxi ride to the college halls of residence; three five-storey buildings named after admirable women: Charlotte Brontë, yes, then Margaret Roper and another of whom she had not heard. A fourth, to make up the square, had been bombed during the war.

Registration was puzzling: where were the men? The offices were full of women, dressed in wide-skirted frocks and cardigans or jackets, just like Joanne wore. She was allocated a room on the second floor where she was greeted by a short, fussy young woman who said, 'I am your college mother and this is my room,' pointing at an open door. The room was large and light, decorated with posters. Joanne noticed some knitting on a chair by a desk, and a duffle bag and a duffle coat with a long striped college scarf on the bed.

'That is a photo of my boyfriend. I see him at weekends, he comes down from Amersham.'

'He's not here at college, then?' Joanne asked.

'What do you mean, here? On a weekday? Men aren't allowed except at the weekend. The men college students are based up in town, in Westminster. Don't worry ... you won't see much of them.'

Joanne contained her panic. She'd never been in a girls-only environment and, from what she'd seen and heard of girls' schools when playing hockey against them, it wasn't one she'd like. She had found the changing room talk petty and the atmosphere claustrophobic and weirdly sexualised, with knowing talk of 'what men like'.

Her own room, along the corridor, was not a room but a small partitioned space with a bed, wardrobe, desk and chair. You sidled down the middle to reach a chest-high window over a small basin. There were four of these 'rooms' on each side of the lino-ed corridor that led to a bathroom, two lavatories and a metal drying cupboard. The whole prospect, inside and outside, was dowdy and the thought of three years there was dreary in the extreme.

Her college mother called her for supper in a downstairs dining room, organised in tables just like school dinners. Afterwards, she was told, there would be a social. The Warden addressed them first of all about 'routines', including the disposal of sanitary towels. She told them she lectured in science and lived in a flat on the first floor.

The social comprised meeting corridor inmates, watching girls smoke and jive, and giving minimal information to such queries as, 'Have you got a boyfriend? Mine lives in Maidstone and works in a bank.'

A solemn group, the Christian Union, sat around the television knitting and watching *Coronation Street*.

Joanne left as soon as she could and climbed the concrete stairs encasing the lift 'for luggage only' and walked along the corridor.

At least the corridor at school had photographs of past school teams where she could pick out her Mother and her Aunt, the man who ran the local garage, and the Uncle who owned the timber yard. All this corridor offered were bossy notices about housekeeping and exhortations to join the Christian Union.

The next morning she was woken by an unusually posh voice calling down the corridor.

'I say, anyone for lax? Lacrosse, they're selecting the team. I'm PJ and I'm going for a trial.'

'Yes,' thought Joanne, turning over in bed, 'a trial it will be.'

School Corridors

As a young teacher in the 1960s, Joanne found corridor duty just about the most tedious of the discipline measures she was supposed to enforce. On corridors they comprised 'not running', 'walking on the left' and, in her words, not hanging about with or without intent. Did these rules secure safety, improve behaviour, increase respect for school life, let alone for teachers? They did not. They simply created another territory for skirmishes between adolescents and young teachers. Mysteriously, the older members of staff did not appear in corridors at lunchtimes, especially during an outbreak of spitting down the stairs that linked upper and lower corridors.

'This needs keeping an eye on,' was the Headmaster's injunction at one of the rare staff meetings. 'It seems to take place outside your classroom, Miss Ebrington.'

Joanne knew better than to point out that hers was the only classroom with a door facing the stairs. It was time for her to call in a favour from one Eddie Sutton, she thought.

She was teaching in her first post in the village where her parents had decided to retire and where she had spent many summer holidays at her grandmother's.

Many days of these holidays were spent playing with 'the gang' – two second cousins down from London, and a few village children of whom her grandmother disapproved. Mavis Sutton, the principal disapproved-of, was Joanne's age, worldly-wise and much put-upon by her pretty, inert mother and her skinny, chain-smoking Dad.

The gang often rode from the station on the goods train to the first level crossing; the cousins and Joanne on the engine footplate, the lesser mortals in the guard's van. Everyone knew it was forbidden but risked a telling-off, or worse, from the mostly invisible station master. It was so exciting to watch the fireman open the firebox and shovel coal into the inferno. Gusts of hot air threatened to scorch their faces as the train clattered along the single track to stop at the crossing keeper's house, drop off the milk churn and wait until the gang had opened the level-crossing gates to block the non-existent road traffic. They then waved to the guard, closed the gates and tramped back along the line.

Another favourite activity was French cricket; fun, yet vicious in tactics. Occasionally, they would play 'proper cricket' against another gang. For this a few more gang members were needed and Mavis's youngest brother, Eddie, would do. They let him bat, knowing he would be out straight away, and put him out to field on the distant boundary where he rarely touched the ball. He was far too young and inept to deserve better treatment.

***

Years later Joanne was given her first form-teacher role in the newly-built high school (a rural secondary modern with a transparently bogus title).

The Headmaster said, 'They had a rather lax teacher last year so they'll need watching. There are one or two trouble-makers ... '

Joanne was not daunted.

On the first morning, she put some flowers from her grandmother's garden on her desk in one of the gold-painted jam jars for which the old lady was famous. The pupils lined up along the corridor.

'Come in, 2B,' and the girls came in, eyeing her carefully. The boys shambled past and settled into the positions of power at the back of the classroom.

'Good Morning, 2B. I have put my name on the blackboard, Miss Ebrington, and I am your form-teacher for this year.'

She heard a low growl as she scanned the register.

''Ere ... I know 'er.'

There was the formal version: Sutton, E. Looking up, Joanne saw a gap-toothed grin, more of a grimace than a smile. It was Eddie.

'Think I'm going to do what *she* says, does she?'

What Joanne called her bat-ears picked up the threat but she chose to ignore it.

The first few days went swimmingly; the class and Joanne were testing each other out. As their English teacher as well as their form-teacher, Joanne chose to read aloud Paul Gallico's *The Snow Goose*, a long short story. She was at the climax of the Dunkirk rescue by the little dinghy, piloted by its crippled owner, when the bell went. Silence; no one moved.

'Well, what happened?' someone demanded.

'We want to know and we ain't going to French until we know,' Eddie insisted.

Joanne realised that the 'power of the story' her college tutors used to talk about was at work on her wary class.

'Tell you what, Miss,' said Ivan, Eddie's small mate. 'I'll go and tell Mr Bates we'll be along soon ... he likes me 'cos my mum's French.'

Before Joanne could respond, Ivan had disappeared. The silence continued.

'He said OK, as long as we all get at least eight out of ten in tomorrow's vocabulary test,' announced Ivan.

'Fat chance!' said Eddie.

Joanne read on.

The class laughed at the expletive from a rescued cockney soldier when the snow goose circled the mast of the little boat. The story's desolate ending in the Fens reasserted the silence in the room. The children picked up their books and quietly left for French. Ivan gave her a thumbs-up and she mouthed, 'Thank you'.

'Pas de problème!' came the reply from the small, dark-haired boy. How did he come to be named Ivan? There was a Polish camp nearby, but that didn't explain things either.

On Thursday, Joanne decided to play her old acquaintance card on Eddie. She asked him if he knew who was spitting down the stairs.

'What if I do?'

'Well, I'd like you to ask them to stop,' replied Joanne in her best school-marmish manner.

No reply as Eddie scuffed away, the fashionable way of walking among the boys.

She was making her way along the corridor to the staff-room on Friday morning, when the Headmaster beckoned her into his study.

'Miss Ebrington, I have to accompany you to your classroom for morning registration.'

'I'm dealing with the spitting down the stairs, Headmaster. I think I've found an ally among the trouble-makers,' she offered.

'Please sit down, Miss Ebrington. This will come as a bit of a shock. It involves a member of your class.'

Joanne thought of all the misdeeds Eddie's gang could perpetrate: freeing the gerbils in the biology lab; electrocuting the tadpoles in their watery nursery; letting down the caretaker's bike tyres.

'There's no way I can soften this,' the Headmaster's voice lowered. 'Yesterday, after dropping the children off at the green in Brailes, the school bus reversed to turn towards Cherington. Some of the boys were pushing and shoving on the verge. Ivan lost his balance and fell into the path of the bus.' The Headmaster paused and looked out of the window. 'His death was near instantaneous.'

Joanne saw Ivan as he was yesterday, chirpily announcing that he'd got ten out of ten in the French test – 'And, 'cos I made him concentrate, Eddie got eight.'

Now she had to face the Headmaster's dry announcement to her class. She had to address an empty chair and desk next to Eddie, and a group of children knowing death in their lives, far from the safety of a tale of distant heroism.

Snapshot 2 ⁑ Measuring

School was about measuring things. Rulers were collected from a pot and everyone rushed to snaffle one that hadn't been hacked by Chris Coe's new penknife.

They had to underline the title and the date then measure things. The class most insistent on measuring was needlework. They even had to measure gingham, which was already divided up into squares that they could count.

Nearly as bad was science – physics, to be exact.

'Get our your lulers and lule a line,' lisped the master over subdued, heartless giggles.

He told them to observe accurately by placing one eye directly above the object.

Joanne just couldn't see what he was on about, let alone focus one eye on the object.

Beside the Seaside

The red-brick market town couldn't have been further from the sea. Midland was an accurate description.

Joanne wanted desperately to live by the sea, even in a bungalow as boring as those her two Birmingham aunts lived in, side by side, in Boscombe, miles from the beach and the smell of seaweed. Her RAF uncle had also retired to Bournemouth, and Joanne had hoped her father would do the same. No such luck when the late 1950s came.

Her family didn't really do holidays. Her father had travelled all over the world in his service career; 'settling-in' was what they did in retirement.

So she perked up when the prospect of a young people's camp in Harlech was announced at the Methodist Youth Club, which she frequented for table tennis rather than its fervent Christian faith. Quickly looking round to see who was signalling interest, Joanne decided they could be companionable, if not as witty as her grammar school friends.

'You'll be in team tents and there will be activities, including talks and prayers.'

'As long as they don't do the "everyone who wants to take Jesus into their hearts come forward" at the end of a discussion of nuclear disarmament,' Joanne thought as she signed the list of possible takers.

A few months later, small suitcases were loaded into Caldecott's only coach and duffle bags stuffed on the overhead racks. Joanne sat near the back with cousin Ruth, whose parents sang tunefully and loudly at the occasional service in Chapel that Joanne forced herself to attend. They also said 'Amen' very strongly at the end of the improvised prayers that rambled on forever with such puzzling phrases as 'and let us bless the empty chair'. It had taken Joanne a while to work out that it referred to Aunt Bessie's recent death.

The long journey to Harlech was relieved by a picnic stop in a lay-by somewhere in Herefordshire. Ruth had a bottle of fizzy Corona, sausage rolls and chocolate marshmallows, while Joanne had a half-sized vacuum flask of tepid tea, beef sandwiches and some bullety jam-tarts. Then there was the challenge of finding somewhere to wee away from the boys and their flamboyant unbuttoning.

Harlech Castle stood on a promontory overlooking the tented camp on a flat field behind the dunes. Camp beds were lined up in large ridge tents and lists of who was in which tent were read out by an officer – in large khaki shorts, an unzipped rain jacket, beige socks, brown sandals and a straggly beard. As Joanne's name was well down the list, she studied the officer and was repelled, judging him to be a prime example of the God Squad whose deliberately softened, patient voices made her want to scream.

The eating and praying part of the camp was in a marquee. The toilet tents were sentry-box shaped and already niffy. The sea lay beyond the dunes with their sharp marram-grass hollows, a much better place to pee, although that risked sudden sightings from wandering groups of boys.

The other side of an asphalt road was a wall with propped bikes and their male riders lounging, eyeing the Methodist newcomers. They looked far more interesting to Joanne than the khaki-shorted officers and the boy-campers. For a start, several of them had dark, Brylcreemed hair, combed back into a DA.

'It stands for duck's arse,' she told timid Phyllis, who was exploring the surroundings with her.

'Oy! How long you here for then?' asked a Welsh voice.

'Just a week.'

'You'll be here tomorrow night then?'

'Yes, but we may have discussion time.'

Phyllis nodded in agreement.

'What's that when it's at home?'

'Oh, talking about things like 'Can you be moral without a religious faith?' or 'Are people like Hindus and Muslims able to go to heaven?'

'Sounds boring ... anyway, see you here tomorrow night.'

'Maybe ... cheerio.'

The boys swung legs over crossbars and rode off towards town. Joanne and Phyllis watched them go and turned back towards the holy encampment, summoned by the supper bell. The long trestle tables and their twin benches were brown and empty, apart from a collection of cardigans where girls had saved sections for friends-but-no-boys.

The meal was very much like school dinners. Queues waited to fill their enamel plates with stew, mashed potato and cabbage. Ruth was a fussy eater, so there was a lot of pushing bits of onion and carrot to the side of the plate. She'd also been told to chew everything thirty-three times, so they were practically the last to leave and read the duty roster for the next day. Breakfast prep for both of them.

The showers at the grammar school had not worked since the war, so Joanne was shy about uninhibited undressing in front of others. She wasn't the only one. There was much wriggling in sleeping bags and wandering off to the toilets in cardigans and skirts over pyjamas.

***

Next day, with swimsuits under outdoor clothes, they made temporary camps in dune hollows and then ran across loose sand to the ridged and solid strip at the water's edge.

Joanne always entered into cold water slowly, but Ruth, normally timid, strode purposefully to swimming depth. Eventually, Joanne was in control of her shudders and swimming with the others.

'Salt water is more buoyant,' Ruth informed her.

'And it tastes funny,' Joanne spluttered as a slightly higher wave struck.

The afternoon was spent playing French cricket and rounders on the camping field. Joanne was good at both; Ruth was hopeless. Swimming was her only physical skill, apart from handwriting and singing. Joanne enjoyed team games and was always one of the first to be picked. At school, Ruth used to offer to be scorer and make neat tables in her spiral-bound notebook.

And so the days' patterns were established, sunny and enjoyable, apart from the evening 'activities'. There was often a sort of service with a couple of jolly hymns, a reading and the interminable improvised prayers.

There were talks and discussions. The only one that drew a full crowd was on 'Boy–Girl Relationships', which everyone hoped would be about sex. It wasn't. It was a joint talk by Mr and Mrs Goodman about how happy they were being married. They were actually excellent table tennis players. so Joanne supposed that helped towards what they coyly described as their 'special secret'.

Escaping from the reverent and stuffy atmosphere of the closing prayers, Joanne made her way to the lounging wall across the road. Sure enough, two teenage boys with bikes were there.

'Hello, going anywhere special?' asked the shorter one. Joanne ignored the question.

'Done anything good today?' asked the other boy.

'Well, yes, sort of.'

'Like what?'

'Swam in the sea, played rounders and French cricket.'

'Is that all?' sneered the shorter one. 'I'd be sure you'd jived all afternoon in the big tent. Did you?'

Joanne looked over his head, out to sea.

'Owen, Mam says you're to come home this minute!' shouted a girl's voice from down the road.

'Sounds like trouble ... you'd best be going. Ta rar!' said the other boy.

'Don't do anything I wouldn't do!' called Shorty as he turned his bike towards the town and its castle.

Joanne rearranged some stones at the base of the wall with her Dunlop Green Flash plimsolls, a reward for being in the school tennis team.

The boy took out a black comb and sleeked both sides of his head. His DA was even more pointed, with a razor-sharp crest. No grammar school boy wore that style. It smacked of rebellion and Bill Haley's 'Rock Around the Clock'.

'What's your name then?' asked the boy, staring out to the dunes.

'Joanne. My friends call me Jo. What's yours?'

'Emirwshcch' was what Joanne heard. 'My Mam calls me Emyr. Do you want to go for a walk tomorrow night, then?'

'OK, but it'll have to be after supper and before lights out.'

'See you at seven.'

'Or a bit later, alligator,' she replied, adapting the latest catchphrase as she caught sight of Ruth and Phyllis bound for the marquee and the evening's earnest discussion of 'Jesus in my life'. Joanne thought she'd rather have Emyr in hers.

On Thursday, afternoon and evening rain rolled down from the hills, grey and gusting There was no Emyr, instead, a sing-song finishing with exhortations to those who had not yet taken Jesus into their hearts to avail themselves of a slot to talk with an officer.

Friday was the last night and there was to be a social. The girls had brought special clothes for it; mainly circular skirts, pale blouses and wide, buckled belts, the best in white patent.

Pale Roman Pink lipstick by Max Factor was applied by all, apart from Ruth, who said she was allergic to make-up. A few washed their hair in the showers; the rest did 100 strokes of the hairbrush to make a shine in already greasy hair.

A couple of the officers sported guitars, the bearded one a washboard, and one of the boys had a side drum that looked as if it had seen service in the Salvation Army. They were expected to dance to skiffle music.

'Impossible,' said Joanne to Phyllis. 'Anyway, most of this lot don't know how to waltz, let alone jive.'

So the girls resigned themselves to an evening of mostly dancing with each other. But at least they could spin round with their skirts swirling out well above their knees.

After a couple of frantic skiffle-rhythm dances, Joanne and Phyllis sat on a side bench, surveying the twirling group with their weird sense of timing, trying to catch the irregular beat of washboard and drum.

Suddenly, outside the tent came the sound of a rock beat and the mid-Atlantic accent of Cliff Richard. It got louder and louder and into the tent came a small group of boys with DAs and a huge portable radio held high.

'Thought you could do with some groovy music,' said Emyr who carried the radio. 'It's Radio Luxembourg's pop tunes time.'

Two or three of the braver girls started dancing. The officers' band went silent and the camp boys shuffled together near the entrance.

Emyr walked over to Joanne, 'Come on, you can do this stuff, can't you?'

'In a while, crocodile,' said Joanne, slowly sipping her lemonade with its slice of orange. Then, assumed sophistication abandoned, she took Emyr's hand, gave her glass to Phyllis, and walked out into the centre.

He was a brilliant dancer. He held her hand gently to guide the moves, none of the pumping grip of the boy-learners. She found herself doing steps she'd only seen in films or as diagrams in girls' comics. He could complement her moves, do ones of his own, and even finish a dance with a coordinated twirl. And a slight bow.

Soon it was nine o'clock. The pastor thanked 'our visitors for their lively music and non-stop dancing' and asked for bowed heads to thank the Lord for the evening. Surprisingly, all complied. The breathlessness in the amen was audible, however.

Then Emyr said, 'Give me your address, will you?'

Joanne ripped a page from Ruth's ever-present spiral-bound notebook and wrote down her address in indelible pencil.

A fortnight later her grandmother called up the stairs, 'Joanne, there's a letter for you. I'll leave it on the table. I'm off down the town.'

Joanne rushed down the steep stairs, brushing past its rough brown curtain. On the table was a letter with her name and address in childish writing.

'Dear Jo I am riting to you from Harlech. Our dance was good. I thort you were pretty. I want to see you beside the seaside soon.'

This was followed by an indecipherable scrawl, the kind Joanne practised on the cover of her rough book for when she would be famous.

There was no address. Joanne felt relieved.

Emyr might have been a good dancer but he couldn't write English. So what on earth could they talk about seriously or argue through, without her winning hands down?

Fig Rolls

Mr Kennett and Miss Innes lived on the corner of Watery Lane and the A34 with its car transporters thundering their way to Cowley.

Joanne thought they led a boring life. Mr Kennett wore a dark striped suit when he wasn't gardening and Miss Innes wafted about wearing lavender and speaking in a soft voice.

Far more interesting were their neighbours, the Lines, a ramshackle family who kept dangerous animals; ferrets who would and did bite through jumper, liberty bodice and vest, leaving two red scars on an eight-year-old's chest.

Joanne had to brave passing the ferret hutch every time she went to play in her grandmother's orchard – a half acre of three fruit trees, a patch of lawn and plants for 'floral arrangements'. The path was common to the Lines and to Mr Kennett, who walked grumpily up to his vegetable garden where he'd smoke his pipe and dig.

'Grumph! Call themselves gardeners? They don't know a carrot from a dock!'

Joanne would try to reply without upsetting a possible overhearer as Mr Lines was not only a volunteer fireman but a prodigious shouter at each member of his family and, possibly, passers-by.

'Mmm,' seemed safest.

One day, sliding quickly past the hutch-of-ferocity, Joanne met Miss Innes wandering up the path towards Mr Kennett's vegetable garden.

'I'm just going to call Mr Kennett for his cup of tea. Would you like to join us, dear?'

Totally confused by this unexpected invitation, and drilled not to be rude to grown-ups, Joanne accompanied Miss Innes up the path, walking on the tufty grass edges while Miss Innes glided along the flat worn earth.

'Tea, Mr Kennett?'

He turned, knocked his pipe out against the fence, and stabbed his fork into the soil. The line of three walked back to the corner house where the child and the man removed their boots.

Their scullery was dark, the hallway was dim, but the living room had two bright bay windows, swathed with patterned nets and framed with crimson velvet curtains.

'Do sit down, dear,' whispered Miss Innes.

Mr Kennett came in smelling of coal-tar soap and sat in the large wing chair opposite Joanne, perched on a little button-back.

Miss Innes brought in a cloth-covered tray with a full set of cups, saucers, teapot, sugar bowl and slop bowl. There were little plates and some curious biscuits, looking like brown church kneelers.

'Do you like fig rolls? They're Mr Kennett's favourites.'

Joanne had never even heard of them, but she nodded politely. Fig rolls were the most unbiscuity biscuits she'd ever tasted; crusty, seedy and strangely sweet in the middle. She much preferred Wagon Wheels.

'What are they teaching you at school, then?' Mr Kennett asked abruptly in his raspy voice.

'Oh, we've just finished doing heraldic shields. And I know how to describe them ... gules, azure, chevron, lion rampant.'

'What use is that?' he demanded.

Joanne hadn't thought that lessons had to be useful, she enjoyed exotic morsels of new knowledge from ex-servicemen teachers, such as the unlikely fact that string vests kept you warm when mountaineering.

Trying to retrieve an equable atmosphere, she offered, 'Well, we did the seven times table last week and I came top in general knowledge.'

A long silence followed while Mr Kennett looked dubious and fiddled with his pipe.

Then Miss Innes gently said, 'I think your grandmother will wonder where you've got to, don't you?'

Joanne stood up, said 'thank you very much for a nice tea' and left as quickly as she could.

***

Five years later, sitting with Mavis Sutton in the old hayloft above the stores of sand and cement, Joanne listened to versions of grown-up sex that sounded highly unlikely to her.

Then Mavis suddenly asked, 'Do you know about that ancient bloke who's a lodger with the old bat down the lane?'

'No, I don't think so.'

'Don't be daft, of course you do. Them two uz lives on the corner.'

'Oh, you mean Mr Kennett and Miss Innes.'

'Yes, that's what I said. Well, me Aunty Nancy cleans at the hospital.'

Sometimes it was hard to resist putting Mavis's logic right, but then she wasn't at grammar school.

'Do you know what I 'eard her say to me Mum?'

Joanne shook her head and leaned forward as Mavis's voice dropped and slowed down.

'The old bloke had a stroke or summat. He was in a bad way. So, they took him to the men's ward … you know, the one that looks across the river.'

Joanne did know, because when you were walking on the other bank you caught glimpses of pyjama-ed figures smoking pipes at the corner of the veranda.

'Well, anyway, the nurses started getting him ready to put into bed, taking his suit off and stuff when he sort-of came round and started shouting at them and trying to clock them one.'

'He can be a bit fierce sometimes,' agreed Joanne, 'specially when he's out of his element.' (A phrase newly learnt in *English Idioms and Sayings*.)

'Out of his element be blowed ... out of his suit, you mean.'

Joanne couldn't get even the drift of what Mavis was on about.

'They had to call one of the porters and a doctor and cart him into a side ward still shouting, me Aunty said. Anyway, next day she goes to the men's ward with her mop and bucket, looks round, no Mr Kennett ... peeps into the side ward, no Mr Kennett.'

Joanne thought Mavis was making a meal out of a common event: someone has a turn, spends a night in the Cottage Hospital, and goes home again.

'Is that it?' Joanne queried.

'No, it's bloomin' not! When Aunty Nancy got to the women's ward there was the corner bed with curtains round it and the rest of the women all quiet in their beds. And do you know why?'

'No, of course I don't.'

Joanne refused to cooperate with Mavis's storytelling ploys.

Mavis took a noisy deep breath.

'Well, it's because Mr Kennett isn't a man. He's a woman. There, what do you think of that? Funny, eh? I mean, after all, men are men and women are women ... they've got different kit, haven't they?'

Joanne made no response. She tried to rearrange her memories, impressions and certainties. Despite his grumpiness, she quite liked Mr Kennett and, as for Miss Innes, she wouldn't harm a fly. But how would they live their contained life with the gossip already circulating?

As usual, her grandmother said nothing, but she must have heard. Joanne couldn't write a letter sharing the mystery with her parents a hundred miles up north.

So Joanne got on with her Latin homework and its three genders (male, female and neuter), she played tennis (singles, doubles, girls and mixed), and read comfortingly of *Little Women*, *Good Wives* and *Jo's Boys*. Sometimes she sneakily glanced at the teenage sex-manual, *He and She*, as it was passed round the class during wet breaks.

A month later, she went round the corner to her Aunt and Uncle's cottage. As she passed Miss Innes' house, she noticed the nets had gone, as had the velvet curtains.

'What's happened at Miss Innes's?' she asked her Aunt.

'Oh, she's gone to her sister's.'

'And Mr Kennett. Where's he living?'

'Didn't you know? No, clearly you didn't. He died in hospital a couple of weeks ago.'

There were many information gaps in Joanne's life. She kept trying to fill them with carefully phrased questions and usually got the sort of reply that was intended to finish the matter.

But she went on thinking about Mr Kennet and Miss Innes and, when she did, she couldn't help remembering the sweet seediness of fig rolls.

Snapshot 3 ✣
Voyages to Camelot

Jack could peel an apple without breaking the curl of skin. His penknife was very sharp, thin bladed, and kept in a top pocket, along with a spare set of keys for the works lorry.

Jack told Joanne that if she threw the peel over her shoulder the letter it formed on the ground was the initial of the prince she would marry.

They would set off to Aston Magna brickworks, or to the stone quarry between Chipping Campden and Broadway. They'd deliver sand and cement on the way there and bricks or stone on the way back.

Jack's brother was a joiner; a rounded, grumpy man who worked with Edgar Maunders in the carpenters' shop.

Edgar once told Joanne that the long empty wooden box on trestles in the middle of the sawdust-strewn floor was a boat. A blunt-ended boat for a little princess with golden locks.

So she hung long shavings in her hair, climbed into the boat and rowed to Camelot.

Edgar smoked silently as he watched her.

Tasting Figs

Joanne had to confess.

'I've tried hard and I can't go!'

So out came the Californian Syrup of Figs. A gluey sweet spoonful was swallowed to relieve constipation, then on to her bike to play in the timberyard, dominated by the huge crane operated by Ernest, the eldest of the Methodist uncles.

Crawling into the gaps between the elm trunks was a favourite part of hide-and-seek; no worry about the seeker clambering over them making them shift and roll.

Another favourite game was to ride the bogey on its railtrack through the stacked planks and leaping off into the saw pit's damp orange sawdust, and London Jack's shout of, 'Oi, you lot, shove 'orf!'

***

Christmas was figs, along with dates and sugared almonds. The half-dried, collapsed figs, with cockeyed stalks, looked like rows of beige berets in their box.

Her grandmother loved them. 'Good for you, too,' she'd say, 'though they do get stuck under your teeth.'

Absences marked grandmother's appearance: few teeth, shapeless ankles, hardly any hair, and definitely no eyebrows.

'I was poisoned!' was the dramatic explanation.

The fish shop had supplied her with some fish that was off and she'd nearly died, was the story. Enhanced by the disappearance of what had been allegedly 'beautiful long hair'.

If she ever were to ingest the smallest fish-related morsel she would die. A temptation for Joanne when, yet again, she'd been forbidden to play with friends dismissed as 'common'.

***

The sexual symbolism of figs marked Joanne's late adolescence. She avidly read D.H. Lawrence, hoping for insights into the mysteries of sexual attraction and the psyche of twenty-year-old men; and to produce a passable essay.

Joanne thought she understood the plot, the characters and even the theme of the chosen novels, but did she understand the symbolism?

The lecturer, terminally boring and shifting from foot to foot as she spoke, addressed the matter. Apparently, it was all to do with how figs were peeled and their appearance during that moment at the dinner table. Was it really so obvious? Or even so banal?

***

Joanne first tasted fresh figs in Morocco. She'd flown to Tangiers on her own, a married woman with two young sons and a husband preoccupied with his art.

She landed in late afternoon. The arrivals hall emptied rapidly, with family welcomes and courier greetings. Of her young au pair, staying with her family nearby, there was no sign. Soon the only figures evident were the customs officials and the occasional taxi driver offering 'a nice hotel for Madame'.

A family group scrambled into the hall, collected in front of her and asked if the return flight to Luton had departed. The runway was empty and Joanne had seen her plane take off again.

'Oh, blimey, we've got problems. Mum was supposed to be on that plane,' said the straw-hatted young man.

'You've got problems? Me too. I'm in Morocco for a fortnight and my hosts haven't turned up.'

Quiet gazing and muttering by mother, son, his wife and two children. Then the young woman touched Joanne's arm.

'Look, we've been staying in a couple of caravans for a month ... there's a spare bunk. Why don't you stay with us until your friend turns up?'

'That's so kind, but how will I ever link up with her, if she comes?'

'Easy. There's a visitors' noticeboard in the arrivals lounge. Write her a postcard. I'll fill in the details of where our vans are.'

Joanne did just that.

After a disturbed sleep and a roll and orange for breakfast, Joanne started to navigate her way to the campsite's washroom.

She noticed a white sports car driving along the sandy tracks. It stopped, the electric window rolled down, a hairy brown arm came out, fingers clenched. Then the up-turned hand opened, to reveal a fresh fig, purple and green, with a pale upright stalk.

'Welcome to Morocco,' an accented male voice said. 'I am Hamid, and a friend of Anissa. I study engineering in Birmingham and I am a Libyan.'

The fig promised good tasting.

***

French-Moroccan families were sometimes disturbing; hospitable and curious, with fixed and strange ideas about the UK.

The first family Anissa, Joanne and 'the leetle Libyan' stayed with lived in Meknes. They'd arrived just before the evening meal.

Soon the adult sons drifted in from work in banks and professional services, immaculate in white shirts and formal suits. They shook hands, mumbled greetings, and ushered their guests into a large bare room, bordered with long, solid cushions. It was occupied by the mother who greeted them effusively.

This matriarch was large, draped in layers of orangy-red cotton cloth that matched her vividly hennaed hair.

The sons soon returned, looking utterly different in their long brown burnouses. Their wives followed quietly in kaftans with wide filigree silver belts. Everyone was served with sweet black tea in tall glasses.

'Anissa tells me,' one son ventured to Joanne, 'that your husband brings you a cup of tea in bed every morning.'

'Yes, he does.'

'Mmmm.'

'And is it true that men can marry each other in your churches?' a younger son eagerly asked.

'No,' she said. 'They can't. Not yet, anyway.'

Again a doubting murmur and Joanne began to feel more and more a foreigner, uncertain of territory, psychologically and ethically.

'Tomorrow we go with the family to a marriage,' said Anissa brightly. 'It's in Fez. But before that we all go to the Hammam.'

Hamid nodded, as did Joanne, who recalled a visit to a Turkish bath at the local swimming pool. The wedding sounded exciting but what were the dress codes, she wondered.

'Anissa,' she whispered. 'I've only brought jeans, summer trousers and T-shirts.'

The phone rang. Answering voices sounded more and more agitated. One of the sons came into the room and said something to the women, at which point the aunts and especially the grandmother erupted into passionate wailing and exclamations, filling the room with high plaintive sounds.

'What's happened?' Joanne asked Anissa.

'The phone call said that one of the other sons has had a car crash with his family. They were on their way to the wedding.'

'What a terrible shock, that's dreadful. Does that mean we won't go to the wedding?' Joanne was secretly glad to avoid the dress dilemma.

After several more minutes of wails and cries and conferences between sons and their wives, the orange grandmother spoke and everything quietened down. Low tables and food in large bowls were brought into the room by the women. Conversation began again.

Anissa interpreted for Joanne.

'Yes, we shall all go to Fez tomorrow.'

Seeing Joanne's puzzled expression she added, 'You see, the accident is a kind of face saver. That son cannot afford the clothes and presents. We all know that, but we must accept what he tells us.'

That was Joanne's first experience of the polite, face-saving lie that throughout her holiday she could never read or anticipate.

Within half an hour everyone was eating.

According to custom, each son in turn proffered fingers holding portions of food. She was glad when she could eat just the figs, selected by herself and in modest volume.

Platform 1

There was only one platform on the station of the small Midland market town. A single track from what the trainspotter cousins called Platform 1, led to Moreton-in-Marsh. There was one train a day on weekdays only, delivering coal for the gasworks, heavy parcels and churns of milk to the level-crossing keepers' houses.

Joanne's mother said she could just about remember passenger trains once a week before the war. The open-fronted waiting shelter had a bench and weeds; the platform had stripes of lumpy blue tiles and, down behind it, a ditch that the gang would clear of nettles to make dens in the low branches of a small oak. From the ditch they had access to the platform and on the other side to a cinder track to the timber yard and The Portable, a shed full of ancient, rusting farm machines.

'Meet at Platform 1 in time for the train,' shouted one of the cousins, newly arrived from London for the summer holidays. Joanne's grandmother disapproved of playing with boys, so a subterfuge was necessary. Girl second cousin, Ruth, lived in Station Road and, although she was a bit boring and a swot, she would provide the alibi.

'Just packing for dressing-up at Ruth's,' Joanne would tell her grandmother, who had the most splendid wardrobe of fancy dresses, including crinolines with metal hoops and, best of all, a black chiffon skirt with swathes of gold- and silver-beaded daisies round the hem. Joanne would never let any friend wear this; it was hers alone. It swirled out when she twirled, which Joanne thought exciting and daring, and a change from mincing up and down Ruth's path in a crinoline, pretending to be a maid-in-waiting to Queen Victoria.

Joanne trudged up the lane with her large suitcase and knocked on Ruth's door.

'I've come to play dressing-up,' she told Ruth's large, neat mother, who always wore a pinny and had her hair in a bun.

'Sorry, dear, but I'm afraid Ruth has got catarrh and can't play today.'

Ruth often had catarrh. She always had dandelion and burdock pop, and Wagon Wheels, but none of those would be shared today.

The alibi confirmed and no lie to be told, Joanna tramped up the road, opened the side gate and walked up the platform slope, leaving the suitcase under the shelter. She could see the boys' bikes propped behind the buffers. Aged ten in the mid-1950s, greeting boys was simple. 'Hello, I'm here. Where's the train?'

'Not come yet, even you can see that,' the elder cousin observed.

The younger cousin, a year older than Joanna, announced, 'Mr Wilson says we can help the guard unload to catch up the time.'

Good, the station master had given them a job so they were 'bona fide', as the older cousin, now at grammar school in London, liked to say.

They could hear the train in the distance. It whistled at the level crossing and steamed into the station a couple of minutes later. The three children approached the engine. The boys greeted the driver and the stoker.

'Oh, you're back for the holidays I see. Come to shovel some coal, have you?'

'Yes, please,' answered the boys.

'I bet you, young lady, want to travel in the guard's van, don't you?'

'No, I don't. Please let me ride in the engine. Please,' Joanne begged.

'We'll see,' said the driver. 'But don't let Mister Wilson see you. He don't mind boys, but girls is another thing.'

The unloading began. A porter's trolley trundled by the stoker into a brick barn, where the children helped to unload cardboard boxes while the coal trucks were emptied by the driver into black shiny mounds for the gas works.

At two o'clock the engine was steaming again for its seven-mile journey back to Moreton, carrying the three children and the three crew, pulling three trucks and the guard's van.

Life on the footplate was hot, busy and cramped with five people. Joanne was wedged against the coal tender and keeping away from the stoker's shovel as he collected and flung fuel into the yellow-hot firebox.

The fields of cows and moon daisies whizzed past. All too soon the train slowed for the second level crossing, where the children got off. The guard off-loaded the milk churn at the keeper's house.

'Right you lot, off you go, and don't forget to close the crossing gates, will you?'

'We won't,' said the boys.

Joanne added, 'Thanks for the ride.'

Walking the mile or so back along the track was fun, striding from sleeper to sleeper, or teetering along the rails themselves. Rounding the last curve before the station, the children spotted London Jack with his dog and stick the other side of the fence.

'Oi,' he shouted, 'Come over 'ere and see what I've got.'

'Not likely,' muttered older cousin.

'Even Uncle Ernest keeps away from him,' warned younger cousin.

'I know who you are, young lady. None o' ye is s'posed to be on the railway. Yer trespassin', that's what yer doin', all o' you. Now, come over 'ere and see what I've got. Alfie won't harm ye. Will ye, Alfie?'

The boy cousins started running over the sleepers; an ideal distance apart for their long legs. Joanne knew she couldn't keep up. She turned towards London

Jack and his quietly growling dog. She climbed over the fence onto the cinder road leading to The Portable and its collection of dusty metal dinosaurs, the long-abandoned harvesters, binders and steam-driven engines. Between the rusting machines were dark places, ideal for hiding.

'Ah, decided to come wi' me, did ye?' asked London Jack. 'Wan' to see what I've got, do ye?'

Joanna said nothing but watched the man warily.

He fiddled in his trouser pocket, deep inside, and pulled out a dirty white handkerchief that bulged damply. 'Here y'are. Somethin' for ye 'cos ye wasn't frit. Close yer eyes.'

Joanne felt trapped, but did as she was told.

'Well, hold yer hands out.'

Unwillingly, she did so, uncurling her fingers slowly. She felt the soft moist bundle.

'There ye are. Open yer eyes. See what I gives yer.'

In her hands, the opened handkerchief revealed the largest mushrooms she had ever seen.

'Ketchuppers, them's called. And only I know where they grows. And mighty good they taste, too, wi' a bit o' bacon. Yer Grandmother loves 'em, I'll be bound.'

Joanne doubted that, but then her grandmother did have some strange tastes; those chitterlings, for a start.

'Well, ye'd best be orf, hadn't ye, and find those scaredy cousins o' yours? Ye can give me the hanky back next time you see me aroun'.'

'Um, I will. And thank you for the mushrooms.'

'Ketchuppers, they are. I told yer, didn't I?'

'Yes, ketchuppers,' she echoed.

Joanne ran down the cinder track, across the ditch to Platform 1. The second cousins were pumping up a flat tyre on the younger's bike.

'Oh, there you are,' said the older. 'We couldn't wait for you. It's supper at six.'

'Yeah,' thought Joanne, but she said nothing.

'What did he show you?' asked the younger cousin, giving a slight smirk.

'Wouldn't you like to know?' replied Joanna, turning on her heel, collecting her suitcase and striding down Platform 1.

'See you tomorrow?'

'Maybe,' said Joanne.

Platform 2

'Mad people' were a source of terror in Joanne's imagination and in her junior school playgrounds. Friends told stories of motiveless murders of children like themselves at the hands of madmen. When these stories echoed in her mind, she could distract herself by staring at something nearby: a vase of flowers; the workings of the window blinds; or the framed black-and-white photographs from before the war hanging on the living room walls at her Grandmother's house.

Her favourite photograph was of some young men from the village stacked up on a ladder propped against a vast bonfire to celebrate the end of World War One. One of these was her grandfather, young, handsome and moustached. John Henry featured only in that photograph. The rest was silence and invisibility. Not even the family building firm featured his name, just his father's, who founded the company.

'Don't talk about your grandfather to your little friends, will you?' Grandma instructed now and again.

'Why would I do that?' Joanne would wonder, knowing nothing.

One day, making a pink blancmange rabbit with her young Aunty Kath, Joanne asked, 'What happened to grandfather; the one standing on the ladder against the big bonfire in Grandma's photograph?'

Stirring the thickening mixture on the stove, Aunty Kath said, 'He's in hospital.'

'Where?'

'In London.'

'Why?'

'Because that's where he has to be.'

'Oh. Does anyone go to visit him? When will he come home so that I can see him?'

'He's not coming home. Grandma goes to see him once a year on his birthday. There, let's pour the mixture into the mould. You hold it steady.'

'Cooee!' Grandma's voice called from Aunty Kath's back door. 'Come and have supper, Joanne.'

So she did, sneaking another look at the bonfire picture as she chewed the reheated beef stew and mashed the potato into the dark gravy.

A week later, Joanne fell out with second cousin Ruth, an only child, fat, fair and clever at school.

'My mother says I'm the prettiest girl in the class,' Ruth announced, sucking on the straw of her school milk bottle.

'Does she?'

'Yes, and my Dad thinks so, too.'

'Well, I don't. And if you don't share your chocolate Wagon Wheel, you'll get even fatter.'

Ruth turned away, flicking her blonde plaits in Joanne's face. They stung her eyes.

'Anyway, at least I haven't got a mad grandfather in a mental hospital.'

Girls in nearby desks turned curiously towards the cousins. The teacher cleared her throat and said, 'After sums, if you're very good, I'll tell you a stowry,' her Welsh accent giving the word a particular magic.

At the end of the afternoon, the class settled down to hear 'The Hunting Hound of Beddgelert': a bloodthirsty story of a faithful dog, slain because falsely accused of savaging a child.

'Done by a madman, I bet,' announced Ruth before the end.

Joanne's tears were in pity for the dog, but everyone thought that she was a crybaby because Ruth had said her grandfather was in a loony bin.

Eating the head of the pink rabbit for tea at her Aunty Kath's, Joanne stirred the topic again.

'Why doesn't my grandfather come home and live with us here?'

'I've told you before. He can't come home. He's in hospital.'

'Can I have the rabbit's tail now? Pink blancmange is my favourite and when I'm grown up and have my own children, I shall give them pink blancmange every day to make them happy.'

'If only it were as simple as that,' sighed her Aunt.

'Anyway, my class were horrible to me on Monday after story.'

'Why? What did they do?'

Avoiding the explanation that would have shown she'd been mean to her cousin, Joanne mumbled, 'They said my grandfather was in a loony bin.'

'Did they, indeed?'

'Yes, and they said I'd catch it too.'

Aunty Kath sat Joanne down, took the empty bowl and licked spoon from her hands, and told her the story of Platform 2.

In her mind Joanne could see the handsome man with a bowler hat, carrying a briefcase, and wearing an overcoat against the cold, waiting for the train at the small two-track mainline station at Moreton.

Staring through the steam as the train drew out, Aunty Kath told her, he could see the fields where his wife's father farmed.

'She should have married a farmer rather than me,' he'd told his younger daughter.

Aunty Kath described how her mother had no way with awkward customers who wanted their building repairs, reroofing and window replacements done immediately, if not sooner. Lady Moya was the worst, and a poor payer, too.

How could her father find workmen to do such jobs when any moment they would be called up to fight in the war?

'There was no way forward that he could see,' Aunty Kath said. 'Things preyed on his mind; he couldn't sleep; he couldn't pay the men; and all the time his tricky wife saying she needed this and that, usually involving a trip to Birmingham in the firm's car, using reserved petrol.'

'What does tricky mean?' asked Joanne.

Aunty Kath stopped staring out of the window. 'Oh, he'd never know what she'd do next.'

Joanne thought, 'Oh, I see. That particular tricky person will tell me again it's none of my business the next time I ask when is she going to see my very own grandfather?'

She could see the stumbling steps of the overcoated figure, with his bowler hat and his briefcase clutched to his chest and a porter approaching him on Platform 2 of Paddington Station. It was like a play.

'Are you all right, sir?'

'Yes, yes. I must telephone Lady Moya, order the paint, get more planks for the coffins, fill the sand store in the stables, send the account to the Council Offices; and goodness knows whether I've got enough petrol to drive the Riley to Birmingham to get her more millinery notions ... '

Shaking his head vigorously, as if trying to avoid a swarm of insects, John Henry was gently escorted from Platform 2.

'Can you give us your name, sir?'

'Mmm?' his eyes engaged vaguely with the ticket inspector. 'No, I don't think I can. But I must return to Platform 2. I've a train to catch.'

'A train to where, sir? Many trains leave from Platform 2.'

'I can't recall the name yet, but it will come if I sit on Platform 2.'

The names didn't return and, after two or three years in the large London Mental Hospital, neither did memory of his wife's face on her annual visit.

He was no trouble, the staff would tell her.

His absence from his wife's life did make trouble. It was shameful and inconvenient. All his affairs were handled by the Court of Chancery and their deliberations were glacially slow.

***

Joanne watched her Aunty Kath staring out of the window, worrying whether her husband, who'd been a promising quantity surveyor, would be able to keep the firm afloat to support her and their growing young family, not to mention his mother-in-law.

'I don't know how your Uncle Ken will manage.'

Tricky Ma had sacked Leonard Slatter, their only decorator, on the spot for refusing to repaint her scullery 'this instant'.

Joanne waited for more information but Aunty Kath was miles away, collecting up the tea things to begin the washing up.

Platform 3

She was rudely fumbled just before the train drew into Platform 3 on York Station; five years later she almost drowned in Switzerland, before returning to Platform 2 at Moreton-in-Marsh.

The half-term journeys to her parents' married quarters at RAF Leeming were a restful relief from the unpredictabilities of life with Grandma.

The bedroom was warmer; no need for the stone hot-water bottle that fell with a frightening thud to the floor in the middle of the night. Meals were on time and tasted good; no rubbery fried chitterlings from the innards of last year's pig, no home-hung bacon with dents where, Joanne suspected, maggots had been cut out. And, best of all, no conversations that could suddenly bring harsh words and condemnations of friends deemed common because they lived in council houses.

At Grandma's, affection was sporadic, promoted by requests for help in sewing that led to rambling recollections of visits to Rose and Albert, who'd moved from the Birmingham suburbs to a bungalow in Bournemouth, only a mile from the sea.

One of the disappointments of 'passing for the grammar' was the weekly afternoon of domestic science; from sewing a gingham apron in the first term to wearing it in the second and third terms for cookery. The whole afternoon was spent in the war-time Air Training Corps hut, cutting out and pinning white bias-binding, then tacking it before finally machining it all round the borders. Mastering the treadle machine meant finishing the 'garment' more quickly, because most girls avoided the fast-needled monster. Joanne was an avoider since the reward for finishing early was the chance to make another garment: a short-sleeved blouse with at least six buttonholes to edge by hand.

Cookery was just as bad; a whole afternoon to make a dish of cornflour mould. Each girl's cookery book contained her laboriously-written recipes done for homework that began: 'Prepare self and lay table. Weigh and measure all ingredients accurately'. Cornflour mould was simply a white blancmange that had to be perilously carried home on the school bus, together with satchel and hockey stick.

Half-term was a relief from the tedium of domestic science.

Dressed in a green tweed coat with a brown velvet collar, Joanne was driven to Banbury Station by her Uncle and accompanied by Grandma, who never missed a chance to shop at the market, no matter how pressing her son-in-law's business was. Joanne had a small suitcase and a red leather shoulder bag with her ticket, hanky and purse holding two shillings.

If they were very early, she could linger by the canal before passing through the ticket office to wait on the platform with its porters and the occasional glimpse of the stationmaster. She had already said goodbye to Grandma who'd replied briskly, 'Well, I must be off. We'll pick you up in a week's time, won't we, Ken?'

The train journey was as usual: smoky drifts past the window; itchy material covering the seats; and the guard, tipped by Grandma, coming past to check that Joanne was still there. She was there all right. Sandwiched between two grown-ups; the man on her left wedged tightly against her and smelling of tobacco smoke.

'How far are you going?' he asked her.

'York,' she answered, trying to shut off any more public questions.

Then he shifted a little, relieving the word-pressure but increasing the bodily. He adjusted his jacket, coughed and seemed to be searching his pocket nearest to her under the formica-topped table. He wasn't searching for a handkerchief, she realised, but had turned his hand round and begun to rub her tweed-covered thigh. Each rub hitched her skirt up a little. Out of the corner of her eye she could see his cheeks shape to a smile.

Panicked, she tried to get the attention of the grown-ups sitting opposite by powerful eye-work. One was reading *The Daily Telegraph*, another was assiduously cleaning a pair of glasses, and the third was asleep, grunting open-mouthed.

'Will you excuse me?' She asked the grown-up on her right. She struggled past the turned-aside knees. No standing up for an eleven-year-old girl.

Along the crowded corridor she soon realised there were no empty seats. No guard to be seen and her suitcase stored on the rack above the smelly groper. She had to return to her seat.

That was when her bomb-proof, hard leather, red shoulder bag became a defensive weapon. Wriggling past the turned-aside knees again, she sat down and wedged the shoulder bag between her thighs and those of the smelly groper. It was uncomfortable but the groper could hardly ask her to move it.

Joanne had learnt her first lesson in silent evasive action. A skill that helped her not one bit when, five years later, Josie tried to drown her in a cold Swiss lake.

***

'I'm thinking of going on the trip to Switzerland with Miss Hill in the summer, ' said Sally, as she and Joanne changed into white Aertex shirts for first team hockey practice.

'Who else is going?'

'It's for sixth form girls only.'

Sally showed no interest in boys, even at seventeen, just sport and her pony. But they were good friends, even though Joanne took Saturday bike rides with David Evans, a year older and planning to be a doctor.

Apart from school teams, Joanne found the sole company of girls dull in comparison with the fun at lunchtimes in the sixth form 'den'. A small store cupboard really, it resonated with echoes of that week's Goon Show: every entrant was greeted with a Bluebottle-chorus of 'Pull up the floor and sit down, Neddy'. Sat on window sill or storage shelves, the group discussed the meaning of life, the putative affairs of the younger staff, and whether they would go to the Easter point-to-point at Springhill or the motorbike scramble on Ilmington Hill. Most people were not interested in horses or motorbikes, they were just a reason to cycle for miles and to spend an afternoon talking about nuclear disarmament, et cetera, et cetera.

That day, the topic in the den was Miss Hill's trip to Switzerland and its outrageous girls-only edict.

Skinny Parker's view was that 'Miss Hill is one of those'. Skinny was always trying to catch up with the latest linguistic codes.

'Don't be daft, Skinny. She's potty about Mr Longdon, any fool can see that.'

'Well, I shall go,' said Jennifer, the only one the school destined to go to Oxford. 'I'm planning my wardrobe already.'

'Blimey, competitive frocks,' Joanne muttered to Sally.

Treacherously, Sally said, 'I'm going too. I want to see the Jungfrau.'

'Just look in the mirror,' Martin Abrams guffawed at his own wit.

Sally went pink and stomped out.

Well, that was it. Joanne offered consolation and solidarity to Sally and they both signed up for the trip.

A month before the due date, the list had twelve signatures and the expedition was on. Mother had pressed the concertina pleats out of her own grey suit and its now-flared skirt and fitted jacket would, she said, be ideal for travelling. Grandmother made a sun top and a gathered skirt from what she called 'a bright print'. Joanne thought it ghastly, with its jungly trees and collected animals, parrots and even elephants, for goodness sake!

With one medium-sized suitcase each, the girls and the sports mistress gathered on the platform in Moreton. Paddington was its usual self and the journey across London and on to the coast, on the ferry and in a long-distance overnight train passed convivially enough. To save expense, no sleepers had been booked and with six in one compartment and seven in the other, they found ways to sleep, taking it in turns to bed down on the seats, the suitcases piled in the aisle and covered with mackintoshes. They even used the two luggage racks, but those were the worst – ridged and covered with metal netting.

As she tried to restore her circulation after a turn on the racks, Joanne stood in the corridor for a while. A young man was also stretching his legs and they talked. He was 'doing psychology at Leicester University' and Joanne was convinced he could read her underlying thoughts with his enhanced perception.

'Enjoy the Jungfrau,' he said as he returned to his carriage. Joanne was sure she had not told him their destination.

She did enjoy the Jungfrau with its rack-and-pinion railway and snow on the peak, and the journey back to the Lauterbrunnen Valley and their homely hotel. The final few days were spent on the shores of Thunersee.

This hotel had a wooden pier, and a platform moored on the lake. A short swim in the cold water afforded a place to sunbathe and to dive. Sally and Joanne were the most enthusiastic to pass time that way.

Jennifer was busy 'protecting her complexion' with Pond's face cream, washing her hair every other day, and shopping for her large and boring elder sister back at home, working in her parents' hotel.

One of their group was Josie, the clumsy daughter of the manager of a local small brewery.

'I can carry a pencil up the stairs under my toes,' she offered one evening at supper. There wasn't much you could say in response to that revelation but Sally and

Joanne sensed Josie's social anxiety and felt sorry for her, so they included her in their before-bed chat.

On the last day, ready for the final swim to the raft Josie stood on the shore in her swimming costume.

'Come and join us,' called Sally.

'I will if you fetch me.'

They swam to the shore. Nearby, Miss Hill was reading her book, wearing huge sunglasses.

'You can swim, can't you?' checked Joanne.

'Yes, but I need you to swim alongside me just to give me confidence.'

'OK,' said Joanne, walking into the water.

Sally and Josie followed and they all slowly swam towards the raft. Josie was doing a curious dog-paddle and Joanne realised she could barely swim. The lake floor plunged steeply and Josie, suddenly out of her depth, grabbed Sally, who sank under the surface, spluttering and flailing. Eluding Josie's grasp she emerged a couple of yards away coughing loudly. That left Josie nearest to Joanne. Her face contorted, Josie reached out and grabbed Joanne's arm. Ferociously strong in her panic, she clamped her arms round Joanne and used her as a human float. Head held under the water, Joanne tried to prise Josie off her back. Josie tightened her grip. Kicking her legs, Joanne managed to surface for a gulp of air and a glimpse of some of the girls and Miss Hill laughing together.

'What a joke! I shall be drowned here in front of everyone,' Joanne thought.

Miss Hill waved and smiled, assuming the girls were fooling about. Then Joanne was under the water again with Josie on top.

Sally had just made it to the bank and realised what was happening. She shouted, 'Help! Help! she's drowning her.'

With her latest desperate gulp Joanne saw Miss Hill run along the pier and dive fully-clothed into the water. A moment later, strong hands turned her over, submerging Josie, who, in renewed panic made a grab for the mistress. Miss Hill pushed Josie under again and shouted, 'Joanne, swim to the shore.'

The rest of the day was spent packing and avoiding Josie, who was proclaiming that her 'adventure' had brought on her catarrh.

Sally, the true friend, shared their adventure in different terms while they waited for parents to collect them from Platform 2 when they got back to Moreton. 'She'd have killed you, you know. Good job I saw you.'

For them, the return to Platform 2 did nothing to wipe out the shared nightmare played out in front of laughing friends.

Tugged and Splintered

Sally Walters was exceptionally tall for an eleven-year-old and had very frizzy brown hair. Joanne knew that she'd have to partner Sally in 'doubles' for the maypole dancing display in the square.

Nobody else wanted to, so Joanne, granddaughter of the owner of the maypole and convenor of the rehearsals, knew she'd be volunteered by her Grandmother. as an act of public kindness.

The maypole had been removed from storage outside her Grandmother's back kitchen and placed in a green-painted oil-drum by the building firm's workmen. Packed with sand and brick, the base was stable enough to cope with being pulled by pairs of dancers on doubled ribbons, skipping in time, over and under the other pairs' ribbons – well, mostly in time – to the tune of 'Come Lasses and Lads'.

As well as being ill-matched in size, Joanne and Sally seemed to hear the rhythm of the song differently. When Sally was at the top of her skip, Joanne's feet were on the ground. They bobbed separately up and down, like sparrows feeding.

'Now then, you two,' shouted the instructor, Mr Wilkes, 'keep together and to the beat.'

He clapped to demonstrate. Joanne was mortified. She was a good solo dancer. 'The Gypsy's Tent', the most complicated dance in the repertoire, had given her no problems. Partnering Sally was a different matter. For a start, Sally didn't say much and she was a clumsy mover at the best of times. By the end of the second rehearsal, Joanne knew she was lumbered with the worst of partners and that yet more practices would be needed with this taciturn, awkward companion.

May Day came and the firm's lorry was decorated with greenery and crêpe-paper roses. Grandmother was also guardian of the May Queen's throne and repainted it each year with her beloved gold paint. Many objects in her house featured gold decoration, including her old wooden sabots, worn when she walked to school in France, 'and a muddy track it was, too'.

While the May Queen and her attendants were being installed on the lorry, the dancers were marched from the school to the square. Summer frocks were mandatory, with sashes of blue and red to make the pairs for the 'doubles' dance.

Grandmother had made each dancer a hairband ornamented with a pair of the crêpe-paper roses. They itched, especially when the dancers got hot. But 'no one is allowed to scratch their heads. Anyone would think you've got nits,' said Grandmother.

The maypole dances did not exactly entrance the spectators, but they were clapped warmly up until the finale: the 'doubles'.

'Come Lasses and Lads take leave of your Dads, away to the maypole high' the music began. Sally's hands were hot and sticky but Joanne joined up to hold the ribbons tightly. On either side of the painted oil-drum, backs to the maypole, sat Grandmother and lorry-driver Jack.

The dance began. The couples had to keep their ribbons taut but some, like Sally flushed with triumph and effort, began to tug as they skipped over and under the opposing pairs. The maypole began to sway. Grandmother and Jack gripped its base to steady it.

The closing bars of the song were coming to their maudlin end when there was a creak, then a sharp crack of timber. Looking up from their dancing, the girls could see the pole bent halfway up and some large splinters of wood splayed out.

'Take your bows,' hissed Grandmother, 'and dance off in your pairs.'

The ribbons fluttered untidily round the broken maypole as Colonel Pride (retired) thanked the dancers for their energetic display of dancing, 'in the true and lively spirit of May Day'.

'True and lively spirit,' muttered Grandmother, 'Those council house children. They don't know their own strength.'

***

Later that summer a zoo came to the small market town. It arrived on the field between the butcher's bungalow and the plastic mac factory, and down from the school. The children were agog.

Each year the school had a zoo trip: a whole day for the infants to Dudley Zoo, while the juniors went to Whipsnade. They agreed that giraffes would not be likely viewing at the zoo down the road as everything had arrived in caravans and closed-top lorries, but they hoped for lions, tigers and, maybe, an elephant.

Piles of poo had been a feature of their previous zoo visits, together with the frightening back and forth prowling of what their teacher had called 'the wild cats'. Joanne wondered how a travelling zoo dealt with their creatures' piles of poo; disposing of her cat Tuppence's poo was enough of a task.

On Saturday morning the zoo opened. It cost sixpence to go in, paid at the desk next to what Grandmother called 'the living caravans'. Across the scrubby grass was a circle of cages, but before that some fenced-in enclosures housed a couple of large goats with thistles hanging from their mouths and a horned antelope munching on hay. The cage circle was in shadow with no labels saying what was to be viewed; not much like a proper zoo, really. The only real match, Joanne thought, was the smell.

'A true zoo smell,' she said to herself, as Grandmother had wandered off to talk to a scruffy looking man with a cigarette in his mouth and eyes scrunched up from the smoke.

Next to the man, with her back to a cage, was Sally, her maypole dancing partner. Over Sally's shoulder, Joanne could see a small shadowy figure with long arms and curled-in hands, a wizened face and golden eyes. It was some kind of monkey that Sally was ignoring, listening to the conversation nearby, although what could interest any eleven-year-old in boring grown-up talk Joanne could not imagine. Puzzling about this, Joanne glimpsed a hand uncurl and reach through the bars. Instantly, Sally let out a scream, 'Let go of my hair! Let go of my hair, you monster!' There she was with her head tugged tight against the cage. The monkey pulled and pulled, harder and harder. The keeper-proprietor was nowhere to be seen and shouting from the grown-ups had no effect.

The next thing Joanne saw was the long arm with a big tuft of curly brown hair held aloft in its fist. Sally was crying in her father's arms, a large bald and bloody patch on the back of her head. The town surgery was just down the road so Sally was carried off, sobbing, for first aid.

'What a silly thing to do, lean your head against a monkey's cage,' Grandmother said. 'Come on, Joanne, we'll get you some nice pink candyfloss.'

***

The last time Joanne heard of Sally was a year later, when they'd both left the primary school to go to nearby grammar schools. Sally was destined for the girls' grammar in Stratford and a hideous uniform of purple blazer, purple beret and black skirt. Joanne's uniform for the co-ed grammar, seven miles in the other direction, was navy, with an embarrassing velour hat for formal occasions and a beret for everyday.

In the 1950s, school transport was limited to there and back at the normal times on weekdays. If you were selected for Saturday team matches you had to bike. Joanne's journey was up and down hills on a minor road; Sally's was along the A34 with its load of car transporters and other large vehicles bound for Birmingham.

They once met by chance in Bradley's, the newsagent and sweet shop, on their way home.

'What's it like at your girls' grammar, Sally?'

'It's all right. Bit boring, really. The best part is on the double-decker with the boys from King Henry's.'

'That's the trouble with going to a girls' school, they get boy mad,' thought Joanne, but she said, 'Well, I must be off. Got English homework to do.'

'We're doing *Midsummer Night's Dream* in English,' said Sally. 'It's weird and we have to learn great chunks of it: "How low am I, thou painted maypole". I knew what that meant at least. Remember your Gran going potty when the thing broke?'

And that was it.

The following Saturday, as Joanne clipped her hockey stick to her bike and filled her saddlebag with the clingy yellow team shirt, navy shorts and socks, and the barely scraped-clean boots, she saw Sally bike past the end of the road with a rucksack on her back. Behind her was the firm's delivery lorry that then turned into the lane.

Jack, the driver, waved and shouted, 'Off for a match, then?'

Joanne wondered why grown-ups asked such daft questions when the answer was obvious. She wanted to reply, 'No, I'm going ballroom dancing', but simply waved back and nodded.

Days later, as Nancy Whale, her Grandmother's neighbour and desultory cleaner, let herself into the house, she called out, 'Is your Grandmother in?'

'No, she's gone down the town shopping. She'll be back soon.'

'Oh, I just wanted to say I'll not be in long this morning. Got to visit Warwick hospital with my cousin, Tony Walters.'

Joanne said nothing, and carried on reading.

'Such a shame, and her in her smart new uniform.'

Joanne wondered why Nancy was going on in an odd voice. The hoover roared its way across the carpet and Joanne lifted her feet to let it pass under the window seat. Nancy switched it off and it did its long deep moan into silence as its bag slowly deflated.

'Your Gran isn't back yet, is she?'

Another pointless grown-up question to which Joanne merely nodded.

'I suppose I'd better tell you then.'

Another nod.

Nancy moved nearer and lowered her voice, 'Sally's had an accident. A bad one. Her dad and me is going to see her in hospital this afternoon by bus.'

Joanne looked up from her book and registered tears in Nancy's eyes.

'She shouldn't have put so much sports stuff in her rucksack. It unbalanced her, see. She fell off her bike and the car transporter couldn't do a thing. She won't know us, or anyone for that matter. But we'll still go, just to keep her company. Severely injured is what they call it.'

Joanne's mouth went dry and her mind recalled the last glimpse of a cyclist at the end of the lane in purple blazer and a matching beret on a mound of frizzy brown hair.

'I'm reserve for the junior hockey team,' the voice had called. 'We're in the County team championships.'

'Reserve is all you'll ever be,' Joanne had thought. Now she blushed at the heartlessness of her thoughts.

'I'm really sorry. Please tell Sally I remember us dancing round the maypole a year ago.'

'I doubt she'll know anything of that,' said Nancy matter-of-factly. 'I don't think she knows anything. Anyway, must go. Tell your Gran the news. And say I'll make up the time next week.'

Several Cycles

Joanne had been given the junior bicycle for her seventh birthday and it was quite the most exciting present she had ever had: her first bike. She thought its name was in honour of the Elizabethan pirate, Raleigh, whose story she'd heard at school that Friday afternoon.

The bicycle was black and shiny because it was brand new, with chrome handlebars and rubber grips that made your hands smell.

Their house was on a little-used road on the RAF station, so that was the place to learn. Daddy was at the end of the road, she'd already practised with him holding the bike at the back. Mummy held the bike as Joanne pulled herself up on one pedal, lifted her leg over to the other pedal and sat on the narrow leather saddle. She wondered why it was called a saddle, surely that was what horses had?

'Go on, Joanne, push off and pedal.'

Mummy let go of the back of the saddle and Joanne put her weight on the right pedal. The bike moved slowly forward, wobbled and fell sideways, carrying Joanne with it. The road hit her knee hard, gravel scratched her shin, and Joanne felt tears welling up with pain and failure.

'Never mind, Joanne, get up and try again,' advised Mummy.

'But my knee hurts and there's blood going onto my sock,' Joanne protested.

'Oh, for goodness sake, don't make a fuss,' was the predictable reply.

Meanwhile, Daddy had untangled her legs from the bike and said, 'Better call it a day, I think.'

Back at the house, Joanne had been consoled with a square of lint and a white bandage and, best of all, the soothing smell of Germolene spread over the lint: pink on pink.

Days later, when a crusty browny-red scab had formed, Joanne noticed a white bump in the middle. She explored it with her fingers. It was hard, a little pale dome.

Mummy brought her the elevenses drinking chocolate. 'Don't pick your scab, Joanne. I'm just off to the NAAFI. You'll be OK? Jock's in the utility room polishing Daddy's buttons.'

Joanne was pleased to have the batman to herself; a chance to find out more about him and to hear his funny way of speaking. Meanwhile there was the white lump to deal with. With a final dig, it emerged: a large round-topped piece of gravel that left a shiny pink cavity. She wondered if it would scar her forever: a badge of bravery after falling off her first bike.

***

Her second bicycle was a Coventry Eagle. It was silver, with straight handlebars, an Indian chief badge below them, and a small saddlebag. Mummy went to buy it second-hand from a house in the nearby town and Joanne was to ride it back the ten miles to the village, on the A34 – a road famous for its car transporters and double-decker buses. She set off after Mummy had reversed out of the side road, tooted, waved and accelerated away.

Joanne couldn't remember a more tiring ride. It wasn't the hilly bits or getting used to gears for the first time. It was the traffic. Every car and lorry in Warwickshire seemed to be on that road, whizzing past and cutting closely in front, one after the other, leaving a whiff of exhaust.

Finally, she reached the top of the familiar hill with its old brewery chimney and brick buildings now owned by her teetotal timber merchant cousins. She coasted down the hill, past the cottage hospital where she'd been born, and turned into the lane where the family was staying with Grandma while their next house 'was being done up, so as Charlie Parker can charge a ridiculous rent', as Aunty Kath had observed.

She leaned the bike against the brick wall of the outhouse, with its dark lavatory used only by Grandma.

'I'm home,' she called, turning the dull brass doorknob.

'Your mother's out,' came the reply. 'And don't let Spot out, he's had his walk.'

Well, that was a relief. Joanne hated taking Spot for a walk. He had a festering growth in one ear, pulled on the lead all the time and, when let off for a run, was deaf to her imploring cries to return. The walk always took twice as long as when Grandma did it – with her piercing whistle and sharp cry of 'Come here at once, you dog'.

***

As well as being a demanding challenge on any bicycle, the Cotswold Hills were ideal for two sports: point-to-points and motorbike trials. Both were favourite haunts for sixth formers from the grammar school. They were events that gave a purpose to cycle rides. They enabled girls and boys to eye each other up and arrange to cycle home together.

They were not as taxing on dress and flirting behaviour as beat dances.

Sporting events meant the chance of a casual meeting, rather than having to endure an excruciating wait before being asked to dance, or the embarrassment of partnering someone who could no more bop than climb a fifty-foot flagpole, or who thought that jive meant never letting go of a partner's hand so you had to twist shoulders awkwardly under a boy's sweaty armpit.

'See you at Oxway Hill on Saturday?' was the invitation.

'Yes, probably,' was the cool reply.

'I've passed my scooter test, by the way. I could pick you up if you like.'

'Oh, OK then.'

'You'll need a helmet. I haven't got a spare. Bye.'

This caused a dilemma. Joanne had never divulged to any adult that she occasionally met boys on her bike rides. She knew no one who had a motorbike helmet she could borrow, nor did she have the cash to get one. Asking for a loan to buy one would result in a cross-examination and she couldn't face the whats, wheres, and whos, particularly the whos.

After supper on Monday evening, Joanne broached the subject. 'Mum, can I have an advance on my pocket money?'

'Why?'

'I need to buy a motorcycle helmet.'

'But you haven't got a scooter, let alone a motorcycle. And anyway they're dangerous. Your father would never let you have one.'

'Mum, I'm not asking for a scooter, just the money for a helmet so that I can ride pillion to the motorbike scramble on Oxway Hill on Saturday.'

'Oxway Hill,' mused Grandma. 'I used to walk there when I was a girl. It had a stone quarry as I recall. Yes, and blue scabious grew there in the summer. I used to pick them to take to Aunt Bessie ... '

Joanne faded out the maundering recollections that required no reply.

'But, Mum, can I have an advance?'

'No.'

'Why not? I passed all my O-levels? Everyone else's parents gave them something for their results.'

'Yes, I know, but your father and I were away visiting Uncle Ted. I tell you what, I'll ask Mr Harvey if his daughter has a helmet you can borrow. You know she's got a scooter now.'

And that was that. End of conversation. Grandma switched on *The Archers*.

Joanne was sure her Mum would forget once she started on the books for Mr Harvey's newsagent business. She was good with numbers and never trusted the mechanical calculator her employer had bought. 'I can do it nearly as quick in my head and sometimes that machine's wrong.' Mum never admitted that she could have punched in an incorrect number.

The next afternoon, Mum came back from work carrying a large dress-shop carrier bag (Mrs Harvey owned Sandra's in the square). She handed it silently to Joanne who pulled out a white helmet with a white peak.

'There. What do you think?'

It was ideal, and white would go with her new cream plastic jacket and pink chiffon scarf: an ensemble Bardot might have worn.

'Oh, Mum. You remembered. You're so kind.'

'Of course I did, and I reminded Mr Harvey about your nine O-levels. He said congratulations, by the way, and said you must take after me, going to the grammar school and such.'

Saturday morning came. The adults had gone shopping and Joanne could take her time getting ready. Especially applying her Roman Pink lipstick and spraying on some of her mother's Chanel No. 5, a Christmas present from Dad.

The light growl of John's scooter stirred Spot into loud barking. Joanne picked up her helmet, locked the back door and saw John standing by the scooter wearing a huge black helmet and goggles.

'Got yours then?'

'Yes, Mum borrowed one for me,' as she tucked her hair behind her ears and fitted the strap under her chin.

'You know those peaks can break your neck if you fall face down?'

'Well, I'm not going to, am I?'

'OK, it's your funeral. Get on board and lean when I do.'

An only child of a divorced mother, John was clever, graceless and attractive, in a lean, fair-haired, pale-skinned with spots kind of way.

Off they went, with John noisily revving the engine, gauntlet gloves grasping the handlebars. Joanne held him tightly round the waist, not sure she was enjoying the experience. They seemed to be going so fast, leaning right and left round bends on the B road to Oxway.

Parking was a casual affair. John propped the scooter up next to a battered Landrover with mud-encrusted tyres.

'You'll have to carry your helmet. It'll get nicked if you leave it on the saddle.'

Joanne was glad her jacket had patch pockets for her purse, hanky and lipstick, rather than having to carry a clutch bag as well as the helmet.

They wandered alongside the hilly track, with its churned-up mud, lingering smell of two-stroke fuel and roar of scramble bikes.

This was her first real date, she suddenly realised.

Many years later, the smell of fuel from her husband's ride-on mower always reminded her of a scooter, a ride over the Cotswold Hills, and the taste of Max Factor's Roman Pink lipstick.

Snapshot 4 ✠ Sunday School

Was there any time of the week so boring as that hour in Sunday School?

Even very slow walking meant Joanne had to arrive eventually at the tin tabernacle. A wartime Nissen hut, presided over by the station padre.

Joanne sat at the end of the row and contemplated the purples, golds and whites draped over the table, flanked by a large silver cross and the RAF insignia proclaiming *Per Ardua ad Astra*. She would mouth this motto in bed at night, fluent in Latin, aged nine.

The best bit, the only good bit, was her very own book into which she could stick her lurid bible story stamps, given out at the end of the afternoon.

The other entertaining element was the race home to change, have cocoa and pick up the proper life of a child: collecting frogspawn, netting for newts and falling out with her brother.

Give Me a Mask

'I know you did naughty things in the built-in wardrobe, didn't you?'

'No, sir, we just played.'

Joanne looked over Leslie's Daddy's shoulder and concentrated on him being headmaster of her school. The rows of books in his study looked boring and shelves of silver cups had blackening splodges. The only object that held her interest was a shiny stone model of a lighthouse, like the one from the Isle of Wight they had in their lounge.

'I know you are not telling the truth, Joanne. I can see it in your face.'

'I am, sir, really.'

'Very well. That's all for now. I haven't finished, but you may go.'

She turned her crêpe-soled sandals on the red and blue rug. It wrinkled but she didn't try to flatten it, she took small steps to the door and carefully turned the brass handle.

Outside, she thought about playing doctors and nurses; a new game that involved taking off jumpers and skirts and being injected on her bottom with a cardboard cone, used for forcing a hyacinth in a winter bulb pot. No one would tell a headmaster about that.

'What did he say?' asked Leslie.

'Oh, not much,' Joanne shrugged. 'My Mummy got a lovely paper fan from the officers' ball, did yours?'

'Yes, we could play Japanese ladies,' Leslie replied, covering her mouth with her hand and blinking slowly.

Joanne thought that didn't look much fun, but at least couldn't involve going to 'The Clinic', taking off clothes, and being questioned and peered at by Leslie's father the next day at school.

That night, in the mirrored bathroom, she practised her still face. She stared at the misty silver surface and mouthed, 'No sir, we just played', hardly moving her lips and certainly not her downcast eyes.

***

Twelve years later, Joanne was at college, training to be a teacher. Actually, she now realised she'd been training to be a teacher for much of her life. Aged nine, she'd run a pretend school beyond the boundary of the cricket field where her Daddy regularly scored half-centuries and took brilliant catches – at least that's what Mummy told her tennis friends. Next to the huge and darkly-shining roller, she'd taken the register of her four-child school, ordered them to sit down after they'd said, 'Good Morning, Miss Ebrington', and told them her favourite story about a brave dog whose reward for protecting his master's child was to be blamed and slain. She was pleased when it reduced two out of the four to tears.

College routines were often as strict and simple, also reducing some to near-tears of boredom. Lectures on 'The Teaching of Mathematics' were conducted in a smiling monotone, explaining the several ways that long division could be carried out. Having passed O-level maths by following numerate procedures rather than by understanding how numbers worked, Joanne struggled to follow the different ways of achieving the right answer in long division.

As she left the lecture theatre from the back row, the lecturer detained her, 'Miss Ebrington, can I have a word?'

Nonplussed, Joanne stopped and smiled.

'I hope when you are teaching a class,' the lecturer muttered (as she gathered her notes together, while Joanne recalled her most recent foray into poetry with a teenage class near Woolwich Arsenal), 'you will not have to endure a pupil gurning and grimacing at you as you try to make clear several methods to solve a simple sum.'

No longer smiling, feeling resentfully blameless, Joanne was shocked into silence. Only afterwards, reflecting on this unwarranted assault, did she realise that her face had betrayed her again, misinterpreted by an unduly sensitive lecturer aware of her own lack of charisma.

Much later, Joanne's own practice of watching pupils' faces to see how they responded and understood, whether they wanted to ask a question or to refute an idea, paid off rewardingly. Fortunately, she never had to teach long division.

***

After retirement from the profession, Joanne decided that she would 'live local'. No more national committees would oblige her to travel from the West Country to debate what and how pupils should be taught, rehearsing arguments so tediously repeated from the 1960s onwards. No more clashes with those convinced that the way they had been taught made them the well-educated and admirable human beings, even impressive politicians, that they undoubtedly were. No more circling obligingly around those whose expertise in university seminars on eighteenth-century prose texts made them decisive about what books, notably Dr Johnson's *Rasselas*, should be read by twenty-first-century adolescents in the UK.

However, she was still interested in professional matters and felt a commitment to progressive practice. So, when it was suggested that she might have something to contribute to the governing body of her local village primary school, she said yes.

Joanne knew by sight some of the people sitting around the formica tables on small-sized chairs for small-sized people. She had, of course, already met the headteacher and his deputy.

'Welcome, Joanne, to your first meeting of the school governors,' said a slim dark-haired woman, pouring glasses of water for her immediate neighbours.

'Ah,' thought Joanne, 'another member of the dehydration police. Anyone would think that the damp West Country offers threats to life like that in the mid-Sahara.'

She'd recently been much amused to see a school group wander into the village square wearing caps with neck guards, parading like a miniature platoon of the Foreign Legion armed with cross-slung water bottles.

The first discussion followed a passionate complaint from a parent governor that 'children are not allowed to leave their seats to get a drink of water when they need to'. Joanne said nothing, but reflected on what a perfect escape ploy 'I'm thirsty' would be for those children bored with the lesson. She had a picture of frequent journeys round the classroom like a fast-forward episode of criminal capture on, say, Paddington Station. No, the notion of school life dictated by 'children's needs' was yet another pointless debate.

Other discussions followed, featuring parent parking, an IT strategy and the latest assessment regime from the DfE. What Joanne had no insight into was actually what the children were learning. Her own primary school experience had been undertaken in five schools, in four different counties, and one different country.

She remembered stuff about dinosaurs, the Romans (repeated in three separate schools), string vests for mountaineers and colouring-in heraldic shields.

The meeting finished after a couple of hours. Two days later, the chair of governors asked her to call at her cottage when she had time.

Sitting in the kitchen she was informed, 'The headteacher said your face told it all. You disapproved of much that was going on in the meeting, apparently.'

'Not at all,' she replied, 'it was all new to me and I was trying to make sense of it.'

'Look, the headteacher said he was not the only one to notice your negative expressions. One of his staff did, and so did another governor who took the trouble to check that I, as chair, was not upset by you peering disapprovingly down your nose.'

'I'm sorry, but they are according me feelings I did not have. I'm short-sighted and was trying to scan the tabled papers and attend to what people were saying at the same time.'

'Well, he insisted that people were upset and thought I'd better tell you.'

'That,' thought Joanne, 'is not the reason I've been summoned here. It's about a headteacher's paranoia and expectations of conformity. Perhaps I shouldn't have told him about the work I did on assessment when seconded to a qualifications authority.' But she actually said, 'Thank you for sharing that with me. I'll be careful not to upset meetings in future by sliding my glasses up and down my nose.'

Joanne laughed and peered at the chair of governors over the top of her glasses.

'This has been so embarrassing,' the chair replied, smiling and sliding her own glasses down her nose. 'Frankly, I think three sensitive souls are making a mountain out of a molehill. You didn't upset me at all.'

'I'll try to remember to put my mask on when I enter the room,' Joanne offered.

'Do that, but tell me what you were really thinking when we have coffee after the next meeting. I'm a social worker and I'm pretty used to subtexts and subterfuge.'

It was then that Joanne decided that being a school governor might be worthwhile after all.

Writing Lessons

Just chalks and rubbers, was how Joanne described the earliest of her lessons in writing.

The mixed infants classroom was long, high-windowed and wooden-floored, with desks and chairs in the top half and gym equipment stored on the left of the bottom half – an assortment of benches, leather-topped boxes and baskets full of balls of different sizes and colours. Their use was totally unknown to five-year-old Joanne. Her school playtime involved only skipping and twirling a wooden hoop around her middle.

After registration, and chorusing 'Yes, Mrs Williams' in the proper intonation, half the class was sent down to the right side of the bottom part of the room. There, at infant-standing height, were small wall-mounted blackboards with curved wooden shelves holding coloured chalks, accumulated chalk dust and board rubbers small enough for little hands.

All Joanne wanted to do was draw a house with a door in the centre and a window each side, downstairs and upstairs, a straight path, and a border of four-leaved daisies running alongside: perfection.

'Take your white chalk and copy the letter "a" for apple.'

Standing, and writing with friable chalk on a vertical surface did not facilitate fine motor skills.

'Now do it five more times and count them on your fingers.'

Dexterity was challenged and the boredom threshold lowered. Soon hands went up.

'Can I go to the toilet please, Mrs Williams?'

'Very well.'

'Can I go too, please Mrs Williams?'

'When Ruth comes back.'

Beyond the heavy door, with its twisted metal ring handle, the asphalt led to the infants' toilets, with green doors that didn't lock and the sharp smell of other infants' unflushed pee. Joanne didn't want to use the lavatory, she just wanted some respite from the tedium of practising letter shapes.

When she got back to the classroom the writing lesson had progressed to "buh" for ball. Joanne knew there were at least twenty other letters to come and an infinity of dullness. Writing lessons were the worst of all the time spent in school, in the view of the mixed infants.

***

'A Snowy Day' was the title of the first composition for which Joanne got a mark higher than five out of ten at her small Cotswold grammar school. Daily English comprised grammar exercises, précis-ing, reading aloud *Rob Roy* or *The Children of the New Forest* round the class, and beginning compositions to be finished for homework. These were an ordeal because you had to 'use your imagination'.

Joanne took that to mean make something up and to invent something completely unknown. This was especially tricky when the title was the likes of 'My Holidays' or 'A Snowy Day'.

Sitting at the living room table after a supper of Heinz tomato soup and a slice of bread (the loaf sawn clasped to Grandmother's chest), Joanne chewed the end of her pencil. Her rough book contained doodles and drawings of women in strapless evening gowns, as well as a few lists, spellings and the workings out of interminable maths problems.

Spot, the smelly old dog, sat at Joanne's feet beseeching her to take him for a walk. This would involve traipsing for miles along the cinder roads of the nearby wood yard, while Spot tore off into the distance, ignoring Joanne's calls. He only responded to Grandmother's piercing whistle.

'I'm off to the council meeting,' Grandmother announced. 'Mind you answer the phone. It could be Lady Moya, and if it is don't say I'll phone back.'

Lady Moya was a demanding customer for the small building firm Joanne's uncle ran. She was the bane of Uncle Ken's life, peremptory and slow to pay.

Joanne rehearsed her script, 'Mr Carter will telephone you as soon as he can. Thank you for the call. Goodbye, Lady Moya.'

Nothing to do but write about a snowy day. What kind of task was that for someone who had begun to wonder about life and its intentions, about whether there was a god, and was John Green in love with her?

Drifting about in her mind, she recalled those times, four years ago, when she was a child living in the centre of Berlin, dragging her solid and steel-runnered sled up the road and past the fir trees at the top, untouched while every second building was a bombed-out wreck. She'd worn red mittens and a red bobble hat, knitted by her mother to keep her warm in the icy weather. And she'd had time to look around at the needled branches with their balanced load of frozen snow. She could still see every detail, including the yellow ring of dog pee by a tree trunk and the thin bent stub of a cigarette.

She quickly wrote down what she saw in her daydream.

Seven out of ten and 'Good, but take care with your spelling'.

***

In the 1970s Jack Holbourne was a big name in writing, for both children and adults. His novels were clever, imaginative and satirical. His illustrated stories entertained kids and grown-ups and were much celebrated by people who taught teachers to teach. Never having taught himself, Jack led experienced teachers into writing for themselves because, 'How could you hope to teach children how to write if you never try to do it yourself?'

The in-service week-long course was in the elegant manor house owned by the County and used for adult education, creative workshops and professional development. Joanne reckoned the one in prospect should encompass all three and was, in any case, a whole week away from 4D, who were a trial at the best of times.

''Ere, Miss. Who's going to have us when you're skiving off?'

'She's a skiver!'

'No, she isn't, but my Dad is.'

'That's not a kind thing to say about your Dad, Sharon.'

'Oh, Miss, not that kind of skiver! He's a skiver at Barratts' shoe factory, and they're top pay.'

Yet another vocabulary lesson from working-class kids in a boot and shoe town: skivers trim leather with the sharpest of knives, she learnt.

Jack Holbourne was diminutive, ordinary looking really, but he wore a turquoise corduroy jacket that said loudly, 'Look at me!' At the midday bar, before the first session began, he sat on a stool, smoking and greeting his course members.

'Hi. I'm Jack. And you must be ... ?'

Each woman introduced herself.

'Fiona.'

'Ah, a Scottish name.'

'Jane.'

'Not a plain one, I see.'

'Liz.'

'Maybe an English queen?'

'Hardly, I'm Jewish.'

'Joanne.'

'Half man, half woman.'

She knew she presented as strong, even though inside she'd always been screwed up with performance phobia, as she called it.

Jack's memorising tags stood him in good stead as the session began in the light-filled room, with its soft chairs and sofas opposite tables with upright chairs fringing the curved walls, and French windows facing the formal garden.

Jack introduced his writing formula: what, where, how.

'Is that it?' thought Joanne.

'I shall give you one of these elements. It is fixed. And then you use your imagination to supply the other two elements to create your highly imaginative story. Alright?'

Most of the twelve nodded.

Joanne kept still, she did not do highly imaginative.

Jack's 'where' was a garden and, by way of encouragement, he elicited first thoughts from group members.

'A garden in space, visited by interstellar astronauts on their way to found a colony on Mars,' volunteered Fiona.

'Great!' said Jack.

'A typical boy's garden with slugs and snails and puppy-dogs' tails,' said Jane, who'd already revealed herself as a Feminist.

'Wow!' said Jack.

'A garden where I can dance to greet the Sun,' offered Liz.

'Cool!' rejoined Jack.

And that was the end of the first session.

Joanne had not been called on to contribute before it was time to unpack, shower and get to the bar before dinner.

She found her room, Honeysuckle, and contemplated the next week with its sisal rugs, beige linen curtains, and resistant single-bed mattress covered with Moroccan-striped blankets. Not to mention the group's uncritical trust in a popular published writer with formulaic ideas about eliciting original writing.

Joanne was first to the bar. She didn't dress particularly carefully, or apply much make-up, but she did put on her heels.

Jack was there, on his stool, now wearing a red leather bomber jacket and black cords.

'Let me buy you a drink, Joanne.'

'Dubonnet. Thank you.'

'I noticed you were a little reticent in the first thoughts part of my introduction.'

'Well, yes. I take a while to acclimatise to new groups.'

'You shouldn't stand back. You should go for it and let your imagination flow. I can help you with that later, if you like.' He smiled and, bafflingly, twirled on his stool.

Into Joanne's mind came the Goon Show rumba of seduction, 'Bloodnock's Rock 'N' Roll Call', aimed at beguiling Spotty Minnie Bannister.

'Maybe, Jack,' she said, as she wandered off to greet fellow heads of English from tough schools and to avoid those who taught in independents.

Joanne turned down the after-supper drinks and began to climb the grand mahogany staircase.

'Hey, Joanne, how about letting your imagination flow along with this wine in my room?' came a playful voice from the upper landing.

He really was a ridiculous little man, Joanne thought.

'I'm sorry, Jack, but no,' and then added without thinking, 'you've stimulated me quite enough already.'

The session after breakfast was a writing workshop. Essentially, everyone was to produce a piece of writing located in a garden. Conveniently, as Jack pointed out, there was a garden outside and the weather was inviting; several group members walked out pensively. Joanne sat at a desk and willed herself into a daydream; nothing came. Then, hearing the American rhythms of Jack's voice stimulating creativity in a young blonde teacher from the local convent school, Joanne remembered an anecdote her North Carolinan brother-in-law had recounted about clipping a hedge in slow motion after smoking hash.

She wrote of this dream-like state, where every movement was slow: the fall of the leaves; the closing of the blades on twigs; time itself.

Then came The Readings. Joanne listened to a scifi space gardener, a parody of Little Bo Peep in a boiler suit, and a story of a dead pet whose gravestone had been discovered in the garden outside. Joanne read aloud her story of suspended time.

After a long silence, Jack began.

'Why did you write this?'

Joanne was flummoxed. 'It was all I could think of.'

'It is clearly a story of castration. I suspect you have a wish to castrate most men you've met, emasculating them.'

Workshop members looked studiously out to the garden and Joanne thought of bolting through the French windows, conveniently open.

'No. It was just an anecdote my brother-in-law told me.'

'Ah, but you chose to tell it.'

Joanne stayed silent and humiliated.

A lesson in writing.

And in reading.

You can never predict what a reader will bring to the text. But you can ignore it, with some difficulty.

Snapshot 5 ※ Family Words

The family loved twisting words and sometimes did so by accident. Narspips were a favourite vegetable and absolute kiosk in the Persian Gulp was mother-in-law's judgement on the Middle East War.

It was she who called Joanne's glamorous Finnish au pair, an oompah girl, in marvellous contrast to the cool style of a six-foot, blonde, blue-eyed presence who caused lorry drivers to swerve and middle-aged blokes to forget how to park.

Family words from mother-in-law also covered financial matters, as in the recall of a time 'when kippers were tuppence a piece'.

Domestic pets suffered from misplaced words. A cat called Penny was male and a ferocious terrier was named Lily.

These transmorphed words held them together, Joanne sometimes thought. Their strangeness reminded them that words were not always what others thought. They weren't permanent. They knew words were elastic, rubber-stretchable, so thin you could see through them.

Meeting Three Poems

Once upon a time in a far off wood
Lived two little pandas gay and good.
One day their Great Aunt Pansy said, 'I think
I'll buy umbrellas for Ponk and Pink¹

This was Joanne's favourite on the occasions when her mother read to her and her brother at bedtime.

The 'Little Grey Squirrel' story was good too, but listening to the rhythm and rhymes of the short poem, together with the adventures of the pandas entranced Joanne. She loved the names, so neat and definite, not like her name, which seemed to fade away; and she'd always wanted an umbrella of her own.

The first time she'd heard the poem was on Christmas afternoon when she was five. The family had had Christmas dinner, which had begun with a glass of sherry for the grown-ups and orange squash for Joanne and Paul. Part way through the meal, which was going on for ages, Joanne pinched her brother's leg that had been kicking her.

'Mummy, she pinched me,' he yowled. 'And she still hurting me.'

'Stop that, Joanne. Immediately, I say.'

'But he keeps kicking me. All the time.'

'That's enough! Both of you.'

'But he did and I hate him.'

There was a silence, followed by a sniff from Grandmother.

'If there's one thing I can't stand, it's spoilt children,' she observed to the home-made paper chain looped across the ceiling.

'Joanne, get down from the table now and leave the room until you can behave yourself.'

She got off her chair, gave her brother a last poke and pulled at the self-closing door to the hallway. It opened slowly and closed behind her with a clunk. She sat on the bottom step of the steep stairs, bordered by their heavy brown curtain, and let her pent-up anger dissolve into floods of noisy tears; it was all so unfair.

He was the favourite, with his blue eyes and fair hair. She was picked on all the time.

For consolation she wound the stair curtain round her. Its harsh bristly surface expressed perfectly the scratchy world she felt wrapped round her. It was cold there, too, with the draught from the front door.

After what seemed ages, her father came out of the living room, smoking a small cigar.

'Are you ready to say sorry to your brother?'

'Do I have to?'

'Yes, you do.'

'But he was kicking me all the time.'

'I know, but he's little and you're big. And anyway, I want you to play the piano for me in the front room. Grandmother has lit a fire in there and we can have tea and Christmas cake. What do you think?'

'Will you read me that panda poem after Paul has gone to bed? Please, Daddy.'

'All right, just this once. You know Mummy really likes to read to you and Paul at bedtime.'

Joanne unwound the curtain and stood up. Father put his hand out. Joanne hiccupped and walked with him into the living room.

'I'm sorry for pinching you.'

'There, that's nice, isn't it, little brother?' said Mother in a squelchy voice.

He said nothing, but smiled sideways at Joanne.

***

> *Up the airy mountain,*
> *Down the rushy glen,*
> *We daren't go a-hunting*
> *For fear of little men;*
> *Wee folk, ...*[2]

Between the ages of five and ten, Joanne went to lots of schools. At least every eighteen months she had to learn the unwritten rules and codes that shaped survival in a new school. This made her a quiet listener, at least for the first month or so in her class. Schools that partly served miltary service camps were used to new children arriving and leaving at any time during the school year. They did nothing to acknowledge the newcomer, apart from a headteacher perhaps saying, 'You will be in Mr White's class.'

In the 1940s there were still all-age schools, with their terrifying 'big girls' and noisy playgrounds dominated by large boys kicking footballs. Teachers were often emergency-trained ex-servicemen or middle-aged women of uncertain temperament and strict routines.

It was a relief to Joanne to find herself one warm June back in her Grandmother's village school – but with a new teacher, Miss Powell.

'Miss Powell is pretty and she wears nice clothes,' Mavis told Joanne as they lined up in the playground before being marched – left, right, left, right – into their classroom.

Mavis was correct. Miss Powell was wearing a white cardigan with embroidered flowers down the front, and she smiled when she said, 'Good morning boys and girls, sit down.'

The hinged double-seats attached to the double-lidded desks made a satisfying clunk as the class lifted their legs and let their weight lower the seats. Round the classroom were a few coloured shiny maps of Great Britain and The World – mostly coloured pink. Some corner-curled art work on blue sugarpaper was left from before the Easter holidays. Classroom display did not feature in teacher-training courses or in a headteacher's expectations.

The day began with times tables, chorused by the class in almost-unison. Because of her erratic schooling, Joanne had gaps in this repertoire and had learnt to mouth silently such challenges as the seven times table.

A spelling list followed, elegantly written in joined-up on a blackboard that had been energetically and dustily cleaned by Chris Coe. He sat in the front row with one of the Brasher twins, whose ne'er-do-well family had been evacuated from Coventry after its spectacular bombing – the glow could be seen in the village, twenty miles away. The spelling list was copied into little grey notebooks to be learnt for homework: a weekly event.

'Now, for a treat,' said Miss Powell. 'We are all going to learn a jolly poem.'

The Brashers curled their lips, Chris Coe stood up for more board cleaning, and Frank Sutton asked to leave the room.

'Please, Miss, it's urgent,' a winning formula.

Miss Powell settled herself on her high wooden chair behind her high wooden desk. She began to read in a low, mysterious voice:

> *Up the airy mountain,*
> *Down the rushy glen,*
> *We daren't go …*

'Clang, clang, clang,' came the sound of a handbell outside the classroom.

'Miss, it's a fire!'

'Thank you, Chris. Now quickly all of you, stand in the aisle.'

They filed out into the playground and stood in their lines: girls first, boys last. After registers were checked, the whistle was blown to end the fire drill and they marched back into the classroom.

Miss Powell began again:

> *Up the airy mountain,*
> *Down the rushy glen,*
> *We daren't go a-hunting*
> *For fear of little men;*

Joanne listened and in her mind's eye she could see the troops of wee folk on their windswept mountain and steep-sided valley. She found it both fascinating and frightening. Goblin was an ugly-sounding word and she was convinced that her world, too, contained such tiny and malevolent creatures; the stuff of nightmares.

She'd spent hours making nests for good fairies and she knew that the dark rings on the lawn were made by the footprints of many tiny beings.

When the poem was finished, Miss Powell said, 'Now, I want you all to make a picture of the poem. Take a sheet of sugarpaper and some pastels from the jars on the windowsills, and make your own picture of the poem.'

Joanne's heart sank. She was hopeless at drawing, she always smudged her pastel colouring-in, and sugarpaper was so rough and in such horrible colours. What she'd have liked to do was march round the playground on her own, saying the poem aloud in a strict rhythm and a menacing voice. Instead, she sat at her desk and drew an orange line on the dull blue sugarpaper for the path the wee folk would take. She made three green humps for the mountains, and some small yellow triangles in the bottom corner for the market tents.

Her picture would not be pinned on the wall, she knew.

***

> *Full fathom five thy father lies;*
> *Of his bones are coral made;*
> *Those are pearls that were his eyes:*
> *Nothing of him that doth fade,*
> *But doth suffer a sea-change*
> *Into something rich and strange.*
> *Sea-nymphs hourly ring his knell:*[3]

Burden

> *Hark! Now I hear them,*

Ding-dong, bell.

The wartime ATC hut, their second-year classroom, filled up after break. The hut was on the far edge of the grammar school field and was the furthest away from the tuck shop: a table in the dining room covered with two types of tuppenny buns known as currants or sugars. School milk crates were near the door with the free third of a pint in their miniature bottles. There were never any sugars left when 2A reached the tuck shop, served by school prefects. Disappointed as usual, the classmates trudged back to their hut.

'It's not fair. You'd think they'd make a system that's fair for all. We ought to be let out a minute early at least once a week,' argued Chick Fowles, whose father was the number two in the maths department.

'Why don't you tell your dad about it?' asked Joanne.

'Don't be stupid. He says that in school we are not family.'

'Sshh. She's coming,' muttered Eric Hodge, door monitor and spy.

The class stood.

'Sit down and open your text book at chapter three, page thirty-one.'

Starting a new chapter held a modicum of excitement: a story, perhaps, or even a scene from a play, before the inevitable comprehension questions and précis exercise. This time it was a poem. Miss Hill read it aloud in a trembling, thrilling voice.

Full fathom five thy father lies;
Of his bones are coral made;
Those are pearls that were his eyes:
Nothing of him that doth fade,
But doth suffer a sea-change
Into something rich and strange.
Sea-nymphs hourly ring his knell:

Hark! Now I hear them,
Ding-dong, bell.

'Now, what do you think it's about?'

One of those huge questions that gave no clues to the right answer, which some of those listening wanted to give.

No one put their hand up.

'A dead dad,' whispered Roger Powell.

The bat-eared teacher picked it up.

'Yes, a father who has been drowned as a result of a shipwreck.'

Joanne thought the man could have been thrown overboard or made to walk the plank, but kept these alternatives to herself.

'Those are pearls that were his eyes.'

Joanne could see the lustrous blank-white orbs and then wondered how the pearls must have drifted out of their oyster shells.

'Sea nymphs hourly ring his knell ... ding-dong.'

What was the word Burden doing there, Joanne wondered. Asked to read the poem aloud, to hear it for a second time, Ruth had included the word Burden.

'No, no. Burden simply means chorus and isn't part of the poem.'

For once, perfect Ruth had got something wrong. She went pink, even on her neck, visible through her plaits.

'Now for homework, you are to learn the poem off by heart for the end of the week. And, for those of you who are in any doubt, that means for Thursday, our last lesson of the week.'

Joanne did not feel doubtful, just disgruntled. It would take ages to learn the poem and she had no intention of missing table tennis at the Methodist Youth Club on Wednesday night.

So, before setting off, still in her school uniform, she sat down to learn the poem off by heart. Such a tedious homework task. What on earth was the point?

Table tennis night was a favourite. Having played for years on a dining room table with a ridge where the extensions were and no space to move back, she was an accurate and fast-reflexed player, specialising in shots that just dropped over the net or looped low to strike a far corner.

That night the leader announced a knock-out competition. Joanne was on form; she beat everyone to reach the final. Much to her father's disgust, she took home a large box of Cadbury's Milk Tray, given to her by the young man whom she had beaten in the final. He was at work and had money, Joanne told her Dad.

'You should not have accepted that gift, Joanne,' said her father.

Joanne was mystified by this but consoled herself by eating a whole layer of the chocolates.

The next day, she tried to learn the poem on the school bus. All she achieved was a deep feeling of queasiness.

The English lesson began. Miss Hill unexpectedly started with the boys' side. One by one they recited the poem more or less accurately. No one failed completely.

Joanne could feel anxiety mounting. She knew the poem by now but 'the dreads' were beginning to manifest themselves. Her breathing became shallow and the world around her shrank in size. She had to pinch her arm to get things back to life-size.

It was her turn.

She stood and attempted to breathe normally so that her voice wouldn't wobble and disappear into an embarrassing sob, the way it had done just before Christmas when reciting 'The People that walked in darkness' in RE. She'd disguised it with a cough, pleading a sore throat. She couldn't use that excuse again.

She decided to pretend to be someone else; a girl with a deeper voice and confident flow. She spoke in this persona, running lines on when needed, ignoring the end-stops that her classmates had employed from learning line-by-line.

There was a short silence.

'Excellent, Joanne. Well-performed. You made it mean something, like a young person would feel after learning of their father's fate.'

Joanne knew she'd have to run the gauntlet of swot and show-off, but she didn't care.

It was enough to have beaten her phobic dreads, for once.

First Infant

Joanne was not cut out for motherhood, or at least the prevailing view of it held by older women.

The school secretary in her tiny tower room up narrow stairs said, 'You must love the rows of white nappies blowing in the breeze. I did.'

Mrs P, the jealous guardian of school stationery, sellotape and, above all, Banda masters for duplication, had had her best days at the end of World War Two.

'I had to swear not to tell anyone that the war had ended until it was publicly announced. Such a responsibility; an honour, really. And me, just in admin.'

Joanne had heard this claim to fame many times before, together with advice on motherhood, but what she really wanted was a box of chalk, some colleague having made off with Room 4's supply.

'Please, Mrs P, can you give me the chalk? 4A will be creating a riot and the HM is on the prowl.'

The year before she'd taken maternity leave from her downtown girls' secondary modern school – a rarity in the 1960s and frowned upon by some colleagues and, of course, by Mrs P. Yet it had been quite a relief to return to the classroom after the statutory two months.

Mother-in-Law was now the live-in weekly help and, providing that she had several gins before supper, the arrangement worked – after a fashion.

Weekends and holidays were spent with husband and little son in a cottage, cold and quiet, in a Warwickshire village forty miles away. They would drop Mother-in-Law at her own cottage in a nearby village then open up their cottage to the peace of an escape from chatter and well-meant suggestions.

Her first infant had been born in the cottage hospital of a small market town. The birth was straightforward, as the attending GP had informed Joanne, looking up from his copy of *The Field*. The nurse had already said, 'All correct and complete.' The little red baby had one eye closed, like a cross little pirate. 'He'll be fine in a short while,' the nurse told her.

Getting back to their weekend cottage was a relief. Joanne was not at her best in worlds run by women; she could not grasp the rules or the modes of conversation with their coded procedural talk.

'Bowels open today?' 'Look at those bee stings round the nipple.' 'Get baby to latch on.'

The small weekend village home was peaceful. Husband at work, painting in the studio. Windows opened to fields and a small garden with a few apple trees and the tangle of a large rose garden, created by a previous owner and only sporadically cared for now.

One sunny day she put her little son into his pram and wheeled him into the apple-tree shade to sleep.

Her husband had gone to visit his mother and, no doubt, taken her to The White Horse for a 'pick-me-up' before lunch.

Joanne settled on the couch to read. Several hours later, she woke, remembered her son as the light and warmth streamed through the many-paned window. Outside, the black pram was outlined in the afternoon sun. The paved path was hot through her slippers. Joanne had not put the pram hood up.

Little infant was still, eyes closed, white sheet transparent with sweat. 'Mother Leaves Son to Bake in Midday Sun' said imagined headlines, 'worse than leaving a dog in a closed car in August'. So she told no one.

She sponged down her little son, who seemed no worse for the experience, and fed him his Farex, which he squelched out of the side of his mouth.

Her second brush with infanticide occurred in the town where both parents worked and lived during the week. She got home early from school and, with Mother-in-Law off to meet an old friend at The Cock Hotel, Joanne decided to wheel the infant in his pram to the supermarket.

Waitrose was a food adventure at that time. Tedious staffroom talk about Martin liking his mussels in garlic cream from the ready-made range was interspersed with the other culinary craze, 'freezing half a lamb bought from a local farm'.

Joanne parked the baby and pram outside the supermarket, collected a trolley and started listless shopping: granulated sugar, salted butter, flours various … what else?

Walking home with her heavy basket, she wondered if Mother-in-Law was aware how competitive her comments on Joanne's domesticity were. 'I wonder you don't darn his socks regularly rather than let them pile up next to the sewing basket,' being the most recent. Augmented by her husband's comment about his socks having 'nests attached', his description of her heel darning.

Opening the blueberry-coloured front door, she called, 'I'm home' to no reply. Mother-in-Law still at The Cock and husband not yet back from college.

She put the basket at the door of the breakfast room en route to the kitchen and caught sight of the baby blanket draped over the newel post.

'Oh Lord! The baby … '

Joanne tore up the avenue, crossed the main road at the primary school's still-flashing beacon, and began the trudge uphill past the small plantation of beech. She turned into the car park and looked over the rows of cars. She couldn't see below the plate window advertisements for avocados, the new deli counter and Extended Opening Hours. No pram was visible.

Weaving between the Minis and the odd Cortina, and sighing with relief, she saw the line of pushchairs and prams. One large, old-fashioned black pram stood at the end of the row with a pair of little feet waving about and a hand-knitted cream blanket draping onto the pavement. There he was, one sock on, one sock off, smiling at the sky.

Occasionally baked and abandoned by mother, infant one was nevertheless a competitive trophy between his grandmother and her neighbour, Vi.

When baby was left in Grandma's care for weekend shopping, Vi would call in for a look and then bear him off to her cottage. Ten minutes later, Grandma would find it necessary to give him his 'elevenses', retrieving infant from 1 Sunnybank to return him to 3 Sunnybank. Within half an hour, Vi would arrive to take baby to see her latest knitted toy, destined for her own granddaughter, whom she rarely saw.

Old Bill, who lived in number 2, was heard to say, 'They pass that baby around between them like he's a ruddy rugby ball.'

Second Infant

Heavily pregnant, Joanne took the bus to the university outreach building rather than walking the half-mile or so of hilly suburb with its run of factories, one boasting 'Foot-shape and Boot-works' in fancy Victorian brickwork.

The University Centre had been a convent, handily next to the Roman Catholic church. It housed a good library, specialising in education, and Joanne had been using the huge oak desks to try to make sense of an ill-conceived survey of adolescent reading tastes. Most of its questions were far too open, reducing any categorisation to an almost impossible task. However, some of the answers relieved the tedium of counting *Little Women,* from the local girls' grammar, and 'anything by Judy Blume' from the girls' secondary moderns. Her current favourite survey choice, maybe a teenage joke,was *Black Busty*, from an out-of-town secondary school, famously near a horse-racing track.

The Centre had a good refectory and some of the seconded university staff were entertaining company at lunchtime. As was a fugitive from the local authority education team who categorised headteachers according to their eccentricities. 'Old so-and-so belongs to the army surplus school of heads. Last time I was there he offered to sell me two pairs of slippers at a special discount.'

In the library, due to close at 3:30, Joanne sensed her time had come. She caught the bus home, walked up the avenue, welcomed her four-year-old back from his nursery school and consigned him to the care of the Finnish au pair, who was willingly and surprisingly staying after her agreed year for the next birth.

Joanne's destination that evening was a maternity hospital in a run-down part of town. Giving birth this time round felt familiar and was accomplished with whiffs of gas and air that had the effect on her brain of several gins in quick succession.

In the early hours in the maternity ward, she surfaced drowsily with the cot bearing her second son beside her. Joanne pulled herself up the tightly-made bed with difficulty and looked around. There were lots of occupied beds and few nurses. Opposite her was a bed with someone looking at a teenage mag. She lowered it to look across at Joanne.

'There, I thought it was you. It's Mrs W, ain't it?'

To Joanne's horror it was an ex-pupil from her down-town girls' secondary modern. Not just any ex-pupil, but a particularly tricky one who had declared, on being encouraged to borrow a library book, 'My family does not accept charity.'

'Oh, hello. Sharon, isn't it?'

'That's right. Want any of my Lucozade? I could bring it across to you and have a look at your babby. Mine hasn't come yet.'

Joanne loathed Lucozade. Her grandmother had dispensed it like the elixir of life every Sunday to ward off 'feeling bilious' and, never feeling bilious, Joanne refused – until forced by an attack of mumps. The fizzy, dark-orange liquid, she judged, would induce nausea rather than prevent it.

She reached over to her little son to fend Sharon off by turning back the cotton cellular blanket to pick him up. Below his mat of fair curls, his little hands clenched and unclenched. He looked just like his older brother had looked on his first day, long and slim. But then Joanne noticed a difference. His right-hand thumb looked larger. He grasped her finger and Joanne saw a pair of thumbs on his right hand looking just like a miniature pink double egg-cup.

She panicked that maybe there were other abnormalities. She rang the nurse bell over the bedhead.

A nurse appeared halfway down the ward, 'Yes, Joanne, what do you want? It's changeover time and I have to be there.'

Joanne couldn't bring herself to shout down the ward, 'My baby has three thumbs!' So, eliminating the panic from her voice slowly said, 'Please come to my bedside. I need help.'

The nurse frowned but moved down the ward.

'Look,' said Joanne, pointing to the hand.

'Oh,' said the nurse, unclipping the notes from the bedfoot. 'We'll be back with you shortly. Don't worry.'

'Blimey! She looked a bit fed up. What did you say?' came the voice from across the ward.

At that point, a nurse in a different-coloured uniform came down the ward, followed by the one Joanne had spoken to. They looked together, not at the little newborn but at the notes. Their low mutters escaped Joanne's ears; Sharon's too, for that matter, who was leaning forward, still clutching her Lucozade bottle.

The two nurses pulled the curtains round the bed. 'We'll be with you shortly. And don't worry.'

The insistence on not worrying spooked Joanne. While her little son closed his eyes in the partial darkness and stopped waving his arms.

A few minutes later, yet another nurse in a navy-blue, and altogether smarter, uniform appeared, followed by an older man redolent with seniority.

They looked at the little child.

'Mmm, nothing in the notes, Matron,' said the grey-haired, dark-suited man.

'No, we were very busy and it was near to changeover time.'

Their frosty exchange finished.

The consultant moved nearer to Joanne. In a quietish but authoritative voice he explained that quite a few babies were born with minor variations, sometimes with genetic origins.

'In fact, the Belgian royal family has precisely this hereditary trait.'

'There's nothing else amiss,' said the matron briskly, 'but initial checks should have been done, recorded in the notes, and you should have been informed rather than having the surprise of finding out for yourself. I must apologise for those omissions.'

Joanne suddenly felt exhausted, relieved but exhausted. All she could manage was a feeble, 'Thank you.'

Finding Elisabeth Ann

Not one for New Year's resolutions, Joanne nevertheless decided at last to start her family history research, using a tutor-supported package from the local history group. In early January the door of the town's museum had a CLOSED sign hanging behind its large glass panes. Then the outline of her tutor appeared.

'Come in. I know it says "Closed" but it stops us being interrupted by people wanting the public lavatories.'

She had listed the family history strand she wanted to sort out: family legends about her grandmother's parentage; the mysterious gift of a farm lease; bastardy with an aristocratic knot; and gaps galore. These were a verbal version of the grubby lace tippet, holey but stylish, she found in the dressing-up trunk full of her grandmother's cast-offs.

Census returns were located, summarised in paid-for family history websites. The tutor could even summon an image of the original documents.

'That signature would be your great-grandfather's as the householder. And there's your grandmother, Alice Mary.'

Richard Collier, her father, had a fair hand, readable and regular, for an 'Estate Labourer' in 1901.

1901

'Pa, there's someone at the door.'

'Well, answer it, my girl. You're nearby, ain't you?'

Alice Mary lifted the latch in the dark doorway of Blenheim Farm. She saw the outline of a tall hat and the hunched shoulders of someone wrapped against the cold.

'Good morning, young lady. Is the head of the household in?'

'My Pa's here if that's who you mean.'

She read the nod and called, 'Pa, a gentleman for you.'

'The census enumerator. Good morning to you. I am here on government business, you understand, and I need a little of your time.'

Pa opened the door wider, moved aside, and the enumerator came in, putting his ledger on the table.

'I have to list who is in this house and what relationship they have to you as head of the household.'

'Alice, fetch the others, will you?'

Her mother and older sister were in the back kitchen: a cold, damp place where butter was churned, weighed out and wrapped for those that lived at The Park. Alice's job was to wipe clean the butter-scales and weights. She liked the cool white-and-grey marbled flat top and could read the weights, 1 lb, 4 lbs, stamped 'Crane F Co Wolverhampton'. She was quick at the board school where her aunt was a teacher and called her 'Alice too-clever-by-half'.

She could hear Pa talking to the man and heard the reply, 'Very well then. Daughter, you say?'

Glimpsing Alice

The tutor printed out the 1911 census return, listing Caroline, 26, and Alice Mary, 12.

Richard Collier was living in a village ten miles away and listed as 'retired farmer' with his wife, six years older than him at 74. Alice was single and a 'mother's help', 22, and declared as granddaughter. So who was Alice's mother?

Scrolling backwards to an earlier census, Richard Collier and Elizabeth Greenway had been married for seven years. They had two daughters, Elisabeth Ann and Hannah, and a son, John, only one year old in 1871.

1871

The door of the cottage had nothing as grand as a knocker. The enumerator hammered on the door then removed his rabbit-skin gauntlets.

'All right. I'm a-coming.'

'Oh, it's you Overseer of the Poor. We don't need the workhouse just yet but, maybe the workhouse needs some butter?'

'No, we don't and, anyway, I'm not the Overseer of the Poor today.' The visitor pulled himself up to his not inconsiderable height, *'I'm the enumerator.'*

'And what's that when it's at home?' asked Richard, chancing his brawny arm.

'I am on government business today, not that of the parish, and I'll thank you to cooperate with a representative of Her Majesty.' The enumerator could see the long village street stretching down the hill, with each dwelling to be knocked up and questioned, the answers checked, written up and countersigned. If they were all going to be as vexing as Richard Collier, he'd be lucky to get home in time for tea.

'I have to list the details of everyone living here at the present. There, is that enough information for you?' asked the enumerator.

'Lucky I've just popped back for the churn from The Park then, isn't it?'

Dragon, the carthorse, was chomping the wayside grass, still attached to his small cart with the churn propped up against two others.

'And your wife's name is?'

'Don't be daft, Overseer, you know her name full well.'

The enumerator sighed.

'The head of the household is required to give me the information I request when I ask him or her, or go before the magistrates to be fined.'

'Oh, very well. I'm short of time, so get on with it, Overseer.'

'Enumerator.'

'As you wish. Enumerator.'

The pen scrawled across the paper, giving the name and age of all who occupied the cottage on that given day.

***

Joanne and the tutor discovered that in 1881, the husband, wife and three children had been supplemented by two more daughters. And in 1891, the estate labourer's family included the 'granddaughter' Alice Mary, aged two years.

1901

'My, you're a pretty one,' said the official. *'Long fair hair, just like Alice in the book.'*

Alice shrank behind her older sister.

'And you, Elisabeth Ann. I hear you're going away to work. In service again? It's a pity you were ill a while since when you last moved to His Lordship's London place, wasn't it? London's an unhealthy place, I hear. What with the Big Stink and all.'

'Elisabeth Ann, your mother needs you now in the back kitchen,' insisted her father. *'What else do you need to know, Enumerator? I have to get back to the estate or The Park, as we have to call it now. Forever planting trees, his Lordship is. Useless things, just blossom, no fruit worth eating.'*

'So Alice Mary, the youngest granddaughter is she?'

'No, list her as daughter to the head of the household and I'll sign.'

'Very well, as you say. Good day to you, Richard Collier,' replied the official, placing his ledger for 1901 in the satchel.

Losing Elisabeth Ann

That was the last time Elisabeth Ann appeared in the Collier family's census return. The tutor searched for her name under local parish records of christenings, marriages, even deaths: no trace.

Confirming family legend with census returns proved tricky. Joanne's grandmother, Alice Mary, as matriarch in the late 1950s, had some status as the widow of a prosperous builder but few friends.

A farmer's wife, Mrs Rainbow, used to visit every fortnight for tea and card games, usually rummy played for matchsticks. Her friendship was based on flattery and the receipt of gifts: objects she fancied from Alice's living room.

One of her less flattering comments to Alice, overheard by son-in-law, Ken, was, 'You know, Alice, the older you get the more you look like Lord D.'

Clearly, Alice had told Mrs Rainbow her 'secret'. She believed herself to be the illegitimate daughter of the great family who owned The Park and a London house. She was not the daughter of Richard Collier, but her mother may have been Elisabeth Ann, whom she called sister.

After an hour or so of fruitless searchings in family history sites, Joanne's tutor returned to the 1911 census. There she was, in another Cotswold market town.

Elisabeth Ann (née Collier), aged 36, was the wife of Oliver Gillett, aged 62, an agricultural labourer, with two adult children and two much younger, aged 4 and 1.

1911

'Oliver Gillett is the name and, yes, my wife's name is Elisabeth Ann. Is that all you need to know about we two then, Enumerator? Our supper is on the table.'

'No, Mister Gillett. I have to note your ages too.'

'What does that matter? She's my second wife and a bit younger, that's all.'

'Mister Gillett, I don't make the laws and it has a column in my ledger with the heading "Age".'

'Oh, very well, but just let me close the door. My two older sons are in from work and taking their food. I want mine too and Elisabeth Ann can answer the rest of the questions. Elisabeth Ann!' he shouted.

His wife came out of the kitchen, wiping her hands on her pinny. 'Don't you mind him, Enumerator. He gets tired at his age after a working day. Now, what more do you want to know?'

She spoke quietly and with only a trace of local Gloucestershire accent. Elisabeth Ann had clearly spent time with others grander than herself. More than that, she had a gentle manner and open face, devoid of the simpering of some ladies' maids. As an undermaid at The Park, she had cleaned bedroom fire-grates with black lead, collected dirty laundry, and dusted and tidied the rooms of the sons of the aristocratic and fashionable family.

One day she heard, 'My, you're still something different!'

The voice made her jump.

'Sorry, sir, I thought you had gone down to breakfast.'

'Just come to collect my boots. We're walking the estate to see the new arboretum I'm told.'

Elisabeth Ann stood still, clutching his half-folded nightshirt.

'Well, mind you fold that properly. I might still need to impress.'

He was the one above all she tried to avoid; the one who had pinned her against the wall in the dairy when she had newly come to The Park to milk and make butter. She'd been recommended by her father, labourer and part-time groom. She daren't tell Pa what had happened that first day and Ma had said, 'Nothing'll come out of it. Put him and his deeds out of your mind, my girl, and get on with your work.'

But Ma was wrong. Alice Mary came out of it during that forced stay in London. When Elisabeth Ann returned, her own family was given Blenheim Farm on the estate and a new baby sister along with her.

Some people guessed but nothing was said. Alice Mary played happily near the farmhouse. Her Pa passed top in the veterinary course for grooms, given by an Oxford professor, in nearby Moreton-

in-Marsh, and Ma made the best butter for miles around. Only Elisabeth Ann was discontented with her lot. The one time when she seemed happy was when she played with her little sister, Alice.

Elisabeth Ann left the farmhouse early one spring morning, hitched a ride from a passing cart from The Park, and disappeared from the family's life.

'Where is she?' was Alice's persistent question. Nobody answered. In fact nobody else seemed to notice she'd gone.

Tracing Elisabeth Ann

It took a great-granddaughter to trace her on the internet over 100 years later.

There were still many holes in Joanne's account of Elisabeth Ann, but the last record of her was only a few miles from her family home. She was married to a farm labourer nearly twice her age and the mother of his two youngest children.

Alice never saw her mother after she'd left Blenheim Farm that spring morning, but she pieced together hints and gossip to make a 'secret' to share in her old age to impress Mrs Rainbow and to amuse her sceptical grandsons, Joanne's cousins.

'Well, we did find Elisabeth Ann, didn't we?' said the tutor. 'But the aristocratic father left no recorded trace. Shame really. The birth certificate had nothing where the father's name should be, and the christening record is blank there too. Still, you'd hardly expect his lordship to own up, would you?'

At that point, the Tai Chi class above the museum began and the rhythmic deafening rattle of their warm-up brought the family history research session to a close.

Making Homes

When she was little, Joanne made homes for fairies. They lived near the hedge that bordered the garden and the wood beyond.

Joanne knew that was where the fairies lived because of three things: one, that the pretty and wispy, blue harebells grew there; two, that there was short grass and soft moss around; and three, there were fairy rings nearby. A grown-up had told her that the dark circles in Daddy's lawn were called fairy rings. Joanne guessed that they were made by fairies dancing round and round at night. There were quite a few of these rings, so the fairies must live near and want to stay.

But where did they sleep?

She looked into where the hedge left the ground. It was bare and twiggy; no place for a fragile small body, let alone gossamer wings.

She gazed up at the silver birch trees that forked into branches too high for a tired fairy to fly up to. Joanne guessed that the fairies needed homes making for them as there were no empty birds' nests or spotted red toadstools ready for conversion.

So Joanne made her first home.

It was round, made of moss with twigs stuck in to make the corners of walls. Some feathers from a recent sparrowhawk murder of a blue-tit too slow to fly off the feeder, and some wool untangled from barbed wire, helped its soft invitation to rest weary gossamer wings. It was surrounded by an ivy-leaved garden and had a tiny path of dry sand from the sandpit.

Joanne was pleased with it – and told her young brother so just before bedtime.

The next morning, after the tedious delay of face flannel and toothbrush, she went to see if the home had been occupied. It had. By a large balding teddy bear, leaning sideways. There was only one person who could have done such a deed.

He was eating his Weetabix while Mummy had a cup of tea and a cigarette. He smiled at his sister from under his long blond lashes.

Joanne knew that direct confrontation would bring a telling-off for her and kind consolation to the brother, probably a tube of Smarties, from Mummy.

'Where's Teddy this morning? Hasn't he got up yet?'

'No,' or rather 'Blo' with a spray of cereal.

'Well, he isn't in your bed ... so there! He's sitting on the fairies' home that I told you I'd made yesterday. You put Teddy on it on purpose, didn't you?'

'Blo. I didn't ... '

'Now, you two, stop arguing. And go outside to play.'

Joanne knew there was no justice to be found in Mummy's world, so she walked out through the utility room and closed the door firmly, knowing the handle was too high for the pest – and favourite.

***

Joanne reckoned that one of the cleverest things Mummy did was to make a home every two years when they were posted to a different station.

Their new house was the same, wherever it was in the country. All the furniture and fittings were standard, as were the pots and pans, cutlery and china, even the wastebins, and a batman to clean Daddy's uniform and shine brown lino floors with the bumper: a long-handled thing with a heavy block at the end covered with grey polishing felt. You swung it backwards and forwards to shine the floor.

The batman was sometimes of interest to Joanne. They were low-ranking airmen who worked for an officer, and sometimes unofficially for his wife. Often, they liked to chat to her while they were working.

Moving house day was a matter of suitcases and a trunk or two to be unpacked; fish and chips bought from a nearby village, and the AGA cooker to be lit.

The next day, after Daddy had gone to the control tower, Mummy set about making a home. First of all there was the rice pudding to put in the bottom slow oven to eat for supper; then shopping at the NAAFI. These on-camp shops were all the same, too.

Finally, there were the small things that made home: Knights' Castille soap; Punch and Judy toothpaste; Daddy's shaving kit with its brush, blond bristles at the base and black-tipped. Better than all these were 'the ornaments', that's what made a home, the familiar relics from overseas postings. Framed photographs arranged in the lounge, of station tennis teams, pre-war images of small planes in desert locations, the occasional portrait of mother in evening dress, and Joanne and Paul astride donkeys on the Isle of Wight. And best of all, there were German beer steins decorated with huntsmen and their horses; the favourite played a tune when you lifted it up.

Then there was the etiquette of 1950s social life: calling cards left on a brass plate in the hall and cocktail parties. Joanne loved those, with people asking, 'And who are you?' as she offered plates of devils on horseback and bowls of nuts.

Finally, there were the neighbouring children to find and sometimes organise in den construction, games of garden croquet and dining room table tennis.

The only tricky matters when establishing a new home were learning the hidden rules of yet another primary school:

'No, that's where the big girls sit.'

'Mr White is mostly cross on a Monday morning and throws tennis balls at you if you talk.'

'The headmaster teaches the school choir and we're practising "Nymphs and Shepherds". Do you know it?'

The best thing about one school was going home on the station bus and running home to pee, because the school's outdoor lavatories were holes in a wooden bench with buckets underneath.

***

In the late 1960s, Joanne and her husband bought a semi-derelict farmhouse in one of four villages mostly owned by an aristocratic family, whose own grand house was down Carriage Drive, a half-mile tarmacked road used by local keep-fitters and the occasional flock of sheep being moved to new pastures.

The farmhouse had the date 1562 on a stone lintel above the initials of a long-ago bailiff of the great family. It also had a tithe barn built of the same soft red sandstone which had once housed the vehicles of a small local bus company.

The house had history and it showed.

The kitchen was rudimentary and cold, as an erstwhile dairy would be. The living rooms had inglenooks and ill-fitting windows and, as for the cellar, its wormy door and worn steps showed it might once have served as a brewhouse. Upstairs, the four bedrooms varied in size from tiny to a walk-through en route to the bathroom and final bedroom. The attic was vast and had a splendid wooden floor but was only accessible via a fold-down ladder. That did not prevent the artist husband having two studio rooms up there and the boys laying out their Scalextric race track.

Making the farmhouse into a home involved demolition, initially. First, the rotten back stairs from the dairy had to be removed; then its cracked ceiling destroyed, showering down debris on Joanne and her Dad as they attacked the plasterboard with crowbars. The debris seemed to be an early form of cavity insulation and barrowloads had to be carted out and piled in a corner of the garden. A year later, in the autumn, the heap grew clumps of mushrooms.

Making a kitchen was the priority for a home and Joanne's mother announced on an early visit, 'What this place needs is an AGA.' Joanne agreed wholeheartedly, but knew about their finances.

A fortnight later, Mother phoned to say, 'I've got you a secondhand AGA.' She kept the books for a few one-man builders and one had said that he'd had to take out an AGA that smoked.

'Nothing wrong with it, of course. Those two had more money than sense. I told them that all it needed was a chimney cowl, but they knew better.'

Mother had said she'd like it for Joanne and secured it, including delivery, for a bottle of whisky and a bottle of gin.

Making a home from a ruin had begun.

Playing Tennis

At eight years old, Joanne proudly called it 'Playing Tennis', her voice providing the capital letters. In reality, it was batting a balding tennis ball against the brick wall of the carpenters' shop just up the lane, with a warped racquet that used to belong to her mother.

'Playing Tennis' on a road linking the A34 to Station Road was possible in those 1950s days. The only regular traffic was the firm's delivery lorry, driven by Jack, brother to Ernie, head carpenter in charge of 'the shop'.

If Joanne hit its wooden door too often with her tennis ball, Ernie would come out and ask her to try to hit the wall as he was measuring timber for a coffin. So, avoiding the door was another challenge to her world-record of twelve hits before missing the ball.

Occasional traffic included timber trucks, with their loads of elm trunks, coal lorries coming from the daily goods train, and Uncle Ken's grey Riley saloon to be put away in the garage. The car had a distinctive engine note, a whine really. Joanne could pick it out from Mr Heaton's room, when the class was quietly doing interminable sums.

Joanne also practised her tennis shots on aircraft hangar doors at an East Anglian RAF station, where the family lived in a pre-fab so damp that she once found a newt in her bedroom. The all-age village school did no sports; they just did tedious exercises involving touching your toes, jumping up and down, hopping and star-jumps.

It was a relief in the school holidays to get back to Grandma's in the Midlands and the lane where, aged ten, Joanne was allowed to use the tennis court in the garden belonging to Aunt Bessie – whose other special attraction was an infinite supply of Blue Bird Toffees.

The tennis court could be used when the boy cousins were visiting timber-merchant aunts and uncles. Widow Aunt Bessie was of that tribe by marriage and lived in her bungalow at the end of the village. A long walk when you didn't know if anyone would be there to play against. The wooden pavilion dated from a time before the war, when then young aunts and uncles played mixed doubles in a team called The Woodpeckers.

The court was kept mown, the net winder worked, and there were a few worn balls in the pavilion, with its counterweighted upper front opening and dusty-wood smell. The few spare racquets were even more warped than her own; a distinct advantage to Joanne when playing a worse-equipped cousin. Hitting the ball out of the whole court was penalised by two points, as there were nettles galore both sides and scratchy currant bushes on one short end. Sometimes it took longer to find the ball than to play a whole game. Here Joanne learnt the pleasure of winning by any means.

She went to secondary school already reasonably skilled in forehand and even backhand. It was time she learnt to serve and smash. The PE mistress, who also taught RE, showed all the girls of 1A and 1B how to serve. Intriguingly, her demonstration did not involve letting go of the tennis ball at all. In her summer skirt, pink blouse and crimson cardigan, her sandalled feet were carefully placed sideways to the back line, with enough room to pivot without going over the line. Her right arm went up and her left arm moved to throw the ball.

'Fully stretched, I come down on the ball and it wings its way over the net. See, girls?'

'Yes, Miss Hill,' they chorused.

'Now everyone take up your position on any of the back lines and practise.'

Sixteen girls, spread along three courts, with half facing half, made for tennis ball mayhem. Balls went everywhere: hitting other players; going into the long-jump pit; and onto the cricket pitch, where the boy outfielders watched with amusement, as did Mr Longdon, a new teacher whom everyone thought Miss Hill fancied.

Walking back to the changing rooms with Sally, Joanne grumbled, 'Well, if that's her idea of playing tennis, it's certainly not mine.'

That evening, playing in the lane, Joanne tried Miss Hill's moves. She chalked the net height on the brick wall and began to learn the angle at which to hit the ball. Learning to take a volley as the next shot, she enlarged her range. By the time she was in the second year at school she was in the third couple for matches. She'd regularly beaten both her boy cousins the summer before, and was given a Dunlop Junior Maxply tennis racquet for her birthday.

***

At the age of sixty, Joanne had a stroke: a cruel pun for a tennis player. She was in a neurology ward for weeks but her brain surgery was successful.

Her subsequent encephalitis was siphoned off by an implanted shunt draining into her stomach, and her hospital-acquired MRSA decolonised.

After months of quiet recovery at home, Michael planned an out-of-season holiday in an expensive resort hotel on the Algarve. The springtime flight to Faro was uneventful and, leaving the arrivals hall, they saw George holding up his placard with their names.

He was stocky and smart, dark-haired and smiling. With a slight bow, he said, 'Welcome to the Algarve. I drive you to the hotel.' And so he did, along a motorway with virtually no traffic and bordered in places by almond trees in blossom.

The hotel buildings were distributed around a gently landscaped estate on the clifftop. Joanne and her husband had been upgraded to the presidential suite, the size of a small house with a view of the sea. They were taken there by an electric buggy, passing the pitch-and-putt, several ponds and pools where fountains played, and a six-court tennis complex with a pavilion and shop. A poster offering coaching by the professional, Ronaldo, was displayed.

'Let's book that, shall we?' Joanne asked her husband.

Michael, relieved that they had made it to their first holiday since Joanne's stroke, agreed and, anyway, he was determined to exercise regularly during the week. He really wanted to regain his erstwhile sporting fitness, let alone his body shape.

After a slow and rather indulgent breakfast, they made their way to the courts. Ronaldo was young, looked very fit and smart in his corporate, fitness instructor, casual wear with immaculately white tennis shoes.

Joanne and Michael were in shorts, faded T-shirts, variously coloured, and trainers that had seen better days.

Ronaldo was from Argentina, spoke good English, and, like all the staff, was polite in an engagingly informal way.

'Now we knock up for a little while, yes?'

'Fine,' the couple agreed.

They started gently. Ronaldo had a bucket full of almost unused tennis balls by him on the backline. He delivered easy forehands alternately to Joanne and Michael. Joanne realised straightaway that five weeks in hospital and rest at home with short walks had not been sufficient to enable even modest running to retrieve a ball.

'Shall we play a short game with you two in the doubles marking and me in singles?'

And they started gently again.

'You two serve alternately in the game and I will see what I can hope to improve in your play, yes?'

Michael served, not stylishly but rapidly, usually managing to place the ball in. They had a short rally that included Joanne returning a wobbly backhand.

Then it was her turn to serve. She made a practice movement, not releasing the ball, just like Miss Hill all those years ago. Then she threw the ball up, but not high enough for a stretch so the racquet could descend with accuracy and force. In fact, she missed the ball completely.

'Try again, love. You're out of practice, let alone what you've been through.'

She tried again and missed the ball again. Somehow, her movements just wouldn't synchronise. Something was missing in her head. She knew what to do, but her kinetic memory had gone. With the third ball she tried again, it dribbled to her feet after her racquet moved but did not connect.

Nearly in tears, she said, 'I'm sorry. I can't. I think I'd better go back to the room and have a lie down.'

Michael and Ronaldo said kind things that she couldn't really register as she left the court in the Portuguese sunshine.

Joanne knew that in her future, playing tennis would no longer be part of who she was.

Endnotes

1   *Pink and Ponk*, published 1952 by RM Publishing (see http://thegregorywebblog.blogspot.com/2014/08/a-childhood-poem.html)
2   *The Fairies* William Allingham (1824–1889) (see https://www.scottishpoetrylibrary.org.uk/poem/fairies/)
3   *The Tempest*, Act 1, Sc. 2, William Shakespeare

Lightning Source UK Ltd.
Milton Keynes UK
UKHW010003280121
377798UK00001B/55